I0542514

A Spell of Mirror Magic

Witchy Ways After Forty, Volume 2

Raven Raine

Published by Raven Raine Publishing, 2023.

A SPELL OF MIRROR MAGIC

First edition. October 16, 2023.

ISBN: 978-0473680787

Written by Raven Raine.

Chapter 1

I SPRINTED TO THE ENTRANCE of my new home with my aunt Ruth as soon as the mail thudded onto the wooden floorboards, my heart pounding. After a seemingly endless wait, maybe I'd finally received my results from the witchy correspondence course for my last theory assessment. If I'd passed, I could advance to the practical assessments—and they would be way more fun.

I leaned down, scooped up the mail from the floor and frantically sorted through it while standing. It had to be here, surely.

There were two letters addressed to my Aunt Ruth, one for her boarder, Raven, and one for me, Heather Nicholls. Could this be it?

Back in the kitchen, I plonked myself in a chair, tossed the other letters on the table and ripped into mine. My face fell and my shoulders slumped as the contents revealed themselves. It wasn't the marked assignment I'd been waiting for. Instead, it was a letter from the library notifying me about a fine for an overdue book I'd forgotten to return. Worse, I hadn't even read it yet.

Aunt Ruth navigated her wheelchair into the kitchen, manoeuvring easier now that she was more accustomed to it. 'Did you get it?' she asked, her cobalt eyes sparkling with curiosity.

I shook my head sadly. 'It hasn't arrived yet. I'm worried it's been lost in the mail.' Dammit.

'It might still come, despite our unreliable postal system,' she said optimistically.

'I sure hope so. By the way, you have two letters.' I handed them over to her.

She tucked them into a pocket of her wheelchair with a sigh of resignation. 'Ah, never mind. We can do something practical together on your next day off.'

My aunt was a high-level witch in her own right who'd taken it upon herself to mentor me in my early training, even though she'd had a serious fall about three months earlier. Despite daily physiotherapy, she had made little progress and may be wheelchair bound indefinitely. However, she'd adjusted her life to fit her new physical limitations with remarkable grace and strength.

'Thanks, Aunt Ruth. I appreciate it.' I rose from the weathered chair. The morning light spilled through the windows, chasing away the shadows that clung to the walls. It bathed everything in a soft golden hue that breathed a radiant life into the space.

I switched on the electric kettle, preparing to make drinks. My aunt could do the job more easily with magic, but I found there was something satisfying about making coffee... or maybe it was simply the anticipation of drinking it.

'Pearl should be here soon.' I finished making the coffees and set them on the table. Aunt Ruth's home help was a wonderful young woman employed to help my aunt with her day-to-day needs and take her out on the days when I was at work... although she had no idea what kind of family she had got involved with.

'We're going to the Apothecary's Potions and Scrolls shop this morning.'

I arched an eyebrow in curiosity. 'Really? Does Pearl know what that place is?'

Aunt Ruth shook her head, her eyes twinkling with amusement. 'I don't think so. To her, it's only a curiosity shop for an old lady like me to explore in.'

'Have a great time!' I glanced at the clock and gulped down my mug of coffee. Much as I wanted to stay and chat with my aunt, it was nearly time for me to leave for Chirtlewood House, where I worked as a guide.

I gave Aunt Ruth a big hug goodbye before I grabbed my bag and strode out the door. Thankfully, she allowed me to drive her car because I couldn't afford one of my own. She had bought an old Triumph off the Internet after kids had stolen and destroyed her Renault. I could only describe the state of the vehicle as a functioning wreck because of its age and general condition, but it ran most of the time. She'd chosen not to get it modified for disability access. Perhaps she still held onto the diminishing possibility of regaining complete use of her legs one day.

That was my wish, too.

As I drove to work, my mind dwelled on the tumultuous events of the past few weeks. A few midlife events had shaken my world up like a blizzard in a snow globe.

I found out about my husband's affair with an ex-colleague and separated from him. To add to the drama, I quit my job as a history teacher. My only daughter, Rose, had left home for university in another city months before, so I was now alone. Leaving New Zealand and travelling to the other side of the world was the only way for me to escape the familiar claustrophobic walls of my uncomfortable midlife crisis.

I'd barely arrived in the UK to help support Aunt Ruth when she warned me of impending personal doom. She told me she would die on the forthcoming third of September. I could never coax a definitive answer from her as to why or how she knew this.

As midlife crises go, I was batting way above average.

I didn't regret my brave choices, though I missed Rose and my BFF, Rachel, terribly. Video calls and texts allowed us to stay connected while I adjusted to a new life far from the only home I'd known. But no words could heal the weight of fear of what would come next for my aunt...

My thoughts cleared as I wound my way through the Kingston traffic. My commute took only a few minutes, and it was seldom busy once I'd left the Kingston area. Almost everyone else drove the other way, towards London.

The stone façade of Chirtlewood House came into view, the morning sunlight reflecting off its bay windows like twinkling eyes surveying everything around it. Two wings extended forward from either end of the house, and wide steps rose to the imposing main entrance. The sixteenth-century manor house's extensive gardens sprawled along the banks of the river Thames near Richmond upon Thames. I'd never tire of the sight of that magnificent building.

I parked my car around the back. The cars of my two work colleagues, Lydia and Penny, were already here.

The gravel of the car park crunched beneath my shoes as I made my way to the entrance. Soon, the house would open for tourists.

But it wasn't only visitors and staff who roamed the rooms of the house. A handful of ghosts also made it their home. I'd quickly learned that supernatural creatures are visible to all witches, and I'd become well acquainted with the resident ghosts in the short time I'd been working there.

I walked inside, bracing myself for the throng of people who would soon arrive to learn the secrets of the old historic manor house.

Chapter 2

I COSIED UP WITH PENNY and Lydia in the cramped office at Chirtlewood House. Lydia, mid-forties and a trainee witch like me, in addition to being the head guide, bore a sadness that reflected the weight of the events of the past few weeks. Penny, about ten years older, appeared stern and joyless as usual. She was oblivious to our supernatural world.

The last few weeks had been difficult for us all. We'd experienced a murder at Chirtlewood House, we'd lost a staff member, and now with only three of us to cover the entire manor house, we fought hard to keep up. We were all tired, and chaos often ensued.

A paper bag sat on the table containing Danish pastries that begged to be eaten. We all took turns at buying something for breakfast on the way to work—which meant I sometimes had two breakfasts if I'd spent time with Aunt Ruth before leaving for work. Not that I minded having two breakfasts. I'd been combatting the extra calories with ever-longer walks in Richmond Park, raising my fitness level at the same time as exploring the enormous park.

After eating and chatting for a bit, we left the office and opened up the house for visitors, putting out signs with directions to the various spots in the grounds.

A SPELL OF MIRROR MAGIC

Over the past week, to our surprise, a shuttle bus had turned up most days at opening time with a small group of tourists eager to soak up some history. Today was no different.

'Heather, you take this group through,' Lydia suggested. 'Penny and I will mind the front door and the upstairs.'

I went outside to where the tour bus driver waited with the entry fees for his group. After taking the money and leaving it with Lydia at the front desk, I led the group inside.

The entrance hall was grand, with a black and white floor tiled like a chessboard. The tourists' footsteps echoed in the cavernous space. Cracked oil portraits of past residents hung crookedly on the walls. The subjects peered down on everyone like silent observers passing judgement. Even the walls seemed to possess secret knowledge of centuries past.

'Wow,' a young girl whispered.

'Look at them fancy chandeliers,' a middle-aged woman said.

I guided them through the elegant rooms and regaled them with tales of the past residents and famous guests who had graced the house over the centuries. The visitors' faces lit up when I described how fashion and décor had changed over time and pointed out the period outfits we had on display. The tour group appeared truly appreciative of the beauty and history that surrounded them here.

And in the gloom trailed a shadowy figure. The ghost of Charlotte Deaville, the long-deceased countess of Chirtle, kept a close eye on the group. Though her presence was clear to me, the tourists had no idea she was prowling around behind them.

Upon completing a tour of the ground floor, we returned to the entranceway and headed up the grand staircase. Its steps were concave from the wear of centuries of booted feet.

One of the tourists screamed. Alarmed, I spun around. Had someone taken a tumble?

No, it wasn't that. A young woman stood rigidly by the mahogany banister, her face pale and her arms hugging her body, shivering uncontrollably.

'It got so cold so suddenly,' she muttered, her voice quivering. 'Like I stepped into a freezer or something.'

'These old houses can be draughty,' I said. Behind the tourist, a faint smirk played upon the countess's lips. She had let this woman pass through her, sending chills throughout the unfortunate woman's entire body.

'There's no breeze,' the poor tourist said. 'This cold came out of nowhere.'

'Perhaps you'd best see a doctor,' said the woman who had admired the chandeliers. 'You might be coming down with one o' them nasty viruses.'

I turned and moved on to avoid any further awkward conversation. A mischievous grin spread across my face, despite my efforts to suppress it. Charlotte loved to give house visitors the shivers. I mentally thanked her for making my group's visit truly memorable.

LATER IN THE MORNING, I stood by the front entrance, selling tickets to new visitors. I also kept a close eye on those who were leaving.

A woman about fifty years old with tousled blonde hair, dressed in an old teal blazer and worn slacks, turned into the entrance hall from the passageway and strode towards the front door. A tote bag with a picture of a kitten hung from her shoulder.

I remembered her arriving about an hour before. At that time, the tote bag had appeared slack, as if it was empty.

But now, lumpy bulges pushed out the fabric along the bag's bottom hem, and it emitted a faint rattling with each of her steps. This kind of thing happened too frequently—an unscrupulous visitor might try to take home a 'souvenir' from among the historic items in the house. Unfortunately, we couldn't catch all of them.

In the corner of the room, Maisey, a young girl with a measles-spotted face and wearing a tatty dress or nightgown, gestured frantically to catch my attention. She jabbed a ghostly finger towards the woman's tote bag.

The blonde woman paused, peeked over her shoulder as if sensing someone was watching her, and continued walking quickly towards the exit. That was odd. Did she think someone was observing or following her from the passageway? She couldn't be aware of Maisey unless she was a witch or had the ability to perceive ghosts herself. But she was definitely scooting towards the exit as quickly as possible.

I raced after the woman, desperate to apprehend her before she got away. 'Excuse me, madam, will you open your bag for me, please?'

The woman stopped in her tracks and slowly turned around, her face a mask of haughty disdain.

'Whatever for?' she asked, her voice ice-cold.

'It is our policy to check bags before people leave the building.' Especially if we have reason to suspect something is amiss.

Her nostrils flared in irritation as she opened the bag.

I peered into it curiously and caught a glimpse of two small, rounded objects. Before I had a chance to investigate further, the woman scrunched the top of the bag closed.

'What are those?' I demanded, blocking her path and preventing her from leaving.

'Nothing,' she replied indignantly. 'Just some stuff I picked up at a second-hand shop.' She attempted to pull the bag away, but I held firm.

I reached out to prevent her from passing by, growing ever more suspicious. 'May I take a closer look?'

'No,' she said, her voice rising.

'I insist.' I tried to keep my tone gentle.

She glared at me in stony silence before finally relenting and re-opening the bag. Reluctantly, she showed me the contents.

Two ceramic eggcups lay side by side in the depths of the bag. They hadn't come from a second-hand shop. They belonged on a shelf in Chirtlewood's kitchen.

I frowned with displeasure and extracted them carefully from the bag. 'Well, it appears I've found something that shouldn't be in here.'

The woman took a step back, her own expression turning menacing. 'I found those fair and square. If you don't give them back, I'll scream,' she warned in a sinister tone.

I stared at her incredulously. 'Why on earth would you do that? What nonsense. You tried to steal these. I should call the police.'

Right away, the woman's demeanour changed. Her proud bearing collapsed, and she seemed to sag into herself. 'No, please don't,' she pleaded, her lips trembling and her voice barely above a whisper. 'I must have them. I'm sure they can't be worth much.'

I had no idea if they might be valuable or not, but that wasn't the point. 'You can't take them. They belong here. If everyone took a souvenir, the place would quickly be empty.'

The woman hunched over and peered up at me with such a miserable expression that I felt sorry for her. I took a deep breath. 'Fine. I won't call the police. But I'll put these eggcups back where they came from.' I glared at her sternly before continuing. 'And I don't want to see you here again.'

As soon as I'd finished giving her a warning, she threw her mouth open, and a ferocious scream erupted, as she had threatened. Her eardrum-splitting shriek echoed around the hall. Undoubtedly, throughout the entire house. I half-expected the windows to shatter.

What on earth was wrong with her? If I wasn't holding the eggcups, I'd have clapped my hands over my ears.

Lydia came running into the entrance hall from somewhere. 'What's going on?'

I gestured at the blonde woman, who had stopped for a moment to get her breath back, and lifted the eggcups in my hand. 'This person tried to steal these. I apprehended her.' With some help from Maisey, of course. I acknowledged the friendly apparition with a slight nod in her direction.

The woman didn't even bother denying what had happened any longer. She bolted out of the house and down the steps before either Lydia or I could react fast enough to prevent her.

Lydia grabbed my arm to stop me from chasing after the would-be thief. 'Let her go. There's no damage done.'

'I couldn't catch her anyway,' I said as the woman disappeared into the distance like a gazelle on a caffeine rush. 'My fitness has improved since my operation, but not *that* much.'

Penny hurried down the stairs with a flurry of her skirt, desperate to investigate the commotion. 'What did I miss?'

'A strange woman tried to steal two eggcups,' I said, peering at them, trying to discern if they might be valuable. I very much doubted they were. One of them was cracked.

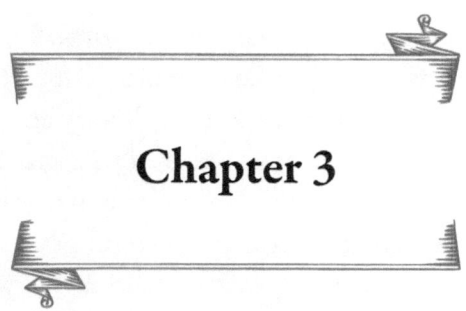

Chapter 3

FIFTEEN MINUTES BEFORE closing time, the phone rang. Still rattled by the strange incident earlier, I picked it up at the front desk. 'Chirtlewood House. Heather Nicholls speaking.'

'Ms Nicholls, this is Inspector Pentecost. I'm calling to let you know that we no longer require the book that was stolen from your library. You can pick it up whenever it's convenient.'

A wave of excitement and relief coursed through me. I'd been desperately waiting for this news! The stolen book was rumoured to be an old witch's spell book containing many secrets and spells of all levels—one of which might help Aunt Ruth regain her mobility.

'Was the book any use to you as evidence?' I asked.

'No.' The inspector's voice was as flat as a pancake. 'We couldn't decipher a word of it.' That didn't surprise me, as it wasn't written in any modern language. 'Anyway, we've got the confession we needed for our case. You can come and take this book off our hands.'

I couldn't help but smile. 'Thank you so much, Inspector! One of us will be there as soon as possible.' And that one of us would be me.

'Who was that? The police?' Lydia asked once I'd hung up.

'Yep. We can get the spell book anytime. I'm going into Kingston after work anyway, so I can pick it up.'

'Great. The sooner it's back in the library and this terrible episode is behind us all, the better.' Lydia glanced around, checking if any of the house visitors were nearby, eavesdropping. The entrance hall was empty.

I pursed my lips and spoke quietly in case anyone entered the room and overheard. 'Actually, I wanted to ask if I could borrow it for a while. I'll take extra special care of it, I promise.'

Lydia squinted at me like I'd sprouted a second head. 'You know that if it's advanced witch magic, you can't yet read it? How's your training going, anyway?'

'I've done all the theoretical assignments. I'm waiting for the last one to be marked and returned.' Damn that slow-moving postal service!

'Same here.' She gave my shoulder an encouraging squeeze. 'Though even then, it might be a while before either of us can make any sense of a high-level witch's spell book.'

'It's for my aunt,' I explained in a hushed whisper. 'She's high level. Maybe it contains an advanced spell to help her heal from the accident that put her in a wheelchair.' Or, even better, save her from dying on the third of September.

'Oh!' Lydia exclaimed, realisation dawning on her face. 'Of course. Take the book. I hope there's something she can use.' She chuckled at some sly thought. 'What will the doctors say if she uses a spell to walk again, I wonder?'

I hadn't considered that until now. All I cared about was making it happen. 'They said it was unlikely she'd ever get movement back in her legs, but they never said it was impossible.'

14

Lydia stared at me thoughtfully before nodding with a smile on her lips. 'Borrow it, then, but don't lose it.'

'There's another thing,' I said. 'I may need to keep it for a little while. Not too long, I promise. If we can find a suitable healing spell, we'll have to wait until her magic mirror is fixed. Without the mirror, her power is greatly reduced.'

Lydia's eyes grew as wide as dinner plates. 'It's broken? How did that happen, if I may ask?'

I winced. 'Um, well, I dropped it down the stairs.' Terrible guilt stabbed through me like a shard of ice.

Lydia glanced around before leaning in closer. 'Can it be repaired?' she asked in a hushed whisper.

Before I could answer, a couple of visitors came into the entrance hall and thanked us. We waited until they'd gone before resuming our conversation.

'I really hope so,' I said with a grimace. Otherwise, my aunt was doomed.

The bell clanged to warn visitors the house would close in a few minutes. Lydia remained at the entrance, while I roamed the ground floor, gathering up stragglers. Penny would be doing the same upstairs.

After we'd closed up the house, I drove to the police station in Kingston, eager to pick up the old tome. The inspector had left it at the reception desk, and all I had to do was sign for it. Delighted, I tucked the heavy, leather-bound volume into the crook of one arm and headed back to the car, ready for wherever the witch's spell book might lead us.

WHEN I FINALLY RETURNED home, I proudly placed the witch's spell book on the dining table like a trophy. Aunt Ruth's super-hot boarder, Raven, swivelled from his study desk in the corner of the room, and his eyes lit up as they met mine. When his gaze fell upon the book, they went supernova.

'Is that the stolen witch's spell book?' he asked, his voice barely above a whisper.

'Yes, it is. But I wouldn't get too excited about it if I were you.' I wasn't being sarcastic; his ex-girlfriend, a witch, had laid a curse on Raven so he turned into an actual raven whenever he became too happy or excited—and it usually took him an entire day to return to human form. It was like being stuck in a horrible avian limbo.

His sudden and—at that time—unexplained transformation had pretty much ruined our first date. And the second date didn't go much better. For now, we'd agreed to put a pause on things until he got the raven-shifting under control.

As curses go, it could be worse, but it was quite a downer when it came to theme parks or sex. Not that we'd had sex, more's the pity.

Raven sighed and raised one hand. 'I'll be completely detached,' he said, though we both knew it wouldn't happen if there was a chance that the book contained a spell to lift the curse on him. The mere idea of that sent a warm glow through me. We could date properly.

Aunt Ruth wheeled into the room and spied the leather-bound book at once. Her head jerked up. 'Is that what I think it is?'

'Yes,' Raven and I replied with uncanny unison.

Aunt Ruth manoeuvred her wheelchair to the dining table as quickly as she could. I'd deliberately left the book where she could roll right up to it. She leafed through the pages, spending several seconds gazing at each before moving on, her excitement increasing with each one.

'I'll cook dinner for us,' I said.

Raven shook his head. 'No need. I made a pasta bake and salad. We're all good.'

I smiled at him gratefully. 'Thanks, Raven.' He really was the best. The only time my horrible ex-husband Terry attempted to cook during the entire time we were together, he made a complete song and dance over it. You would have thought he had cured cancer, instead of simply microwaving frozen mac 'n' cheese.

'No problem. You've been working all day. I've been home, studying.'

Searching for a way to remove the curse on you, you mean.

I headed to the bathroom to freshen up, and then to my room to rest for a few minutes. I'd been on my feet nearly all day and my forty-four-year-old body was feeling it! It was almost three months since I'd had my hysterectomy back in New Zealand. Would the post-op effects ever completely go away?

'Dinner's ready!' Raven called from downstairs. I headed down.

Aunt Ruth pushed the book aside when Raven put a plate in front of her, but not so far that she couldn't still turn the pages. The open pages were clearly visible to me from the other side of the table, though I couldn't make any sense of the symbols, pictograms and cursive script on them.

We all ate silently for a minute or two. Aunt Ruth was so absorbed in the book she only picked at her dinner from time to time. I exchanged glances with Raven. Would she tell us anything?

'Is the writing in another language, Aunt Ruth?' I asked, curiosity piqued.

She glanced up before turning her attention back to the book. 'Most of it is in old English. The rest is in old Danish. I'm not reading it, only skimming. This is an impressive spell book, Heather. We must make a copy of it when we can.'

'When we have got your magic mirror fixed so you can cast the spell. I know.'

She turned her attention back to the book, her dinner forgotten for now.

I finished eating. Beside me, Raven laid his cutlery on his empty plate. I stood, gathered our plates, took them into the kitchen and placed them in the dishwasher with a clang. Raven's voice sounded from the dining room, asking Aunt Ruth if she hadn't liked the pasta bake.

I returned to the dining room with steaming mugs of tea and coffee and set one in front of each of us. Aunt Ruth was eating her dinner now, but she still flipped the pages.

'Have you found any healing spells?' My curiosity wouldn't let me wait any longer, but I didn't want to pressure my aunt by us sitting around her like a group of hungry lions ready to pounce on their prey.

She looked up, smiling knowingly. 'Yes. There are several. Most are for curing illnesses, so they won't help me, but there is one other that might. It's impossible to be sure, because at the time the spell was written...' She shrugged.

'People didn't understand much about anatomy and physiology back then,' Raven said.

'Exactly. But it is for self-healing broken bones,' Aunt Ruth said with a small chuckle, 'so it might be effective, or perhaps I can enhance it to make it work.'

I leaned forward in my seat, my excitement growing with every word they said. 'Hold on a second. That's for self-healing. Are there spells to heal others in there? Could a powerful witch heal you, Aunt Ruth? Then we wouldn't have to wait for the mirror to be fixed.'

She stared at me for a few moments, as if unsure what to say. Or maybe she simply didn't want to say it. 'Spells to heal others do exist, but they can only be used when the spellcaster can see what they're doing. If they don't know what's going on inside the body, the healing spell could actually make things worse.'

I processed her words. So, no blind castings. Got it. 'But if you knew a surgeon or doctor who had access to the CT scans, MRIs and X-rays,' I continued, my excitement growing again. 'And who was also a witch or a warlock—'

'A witchdoctor,' Raven said. His lips quirked up in amusement.

Aunt Ruth shrugged. 'Maybe, but I've never heard of anyone like that. I doubt they'd advertise their services on the Witchnet. Professional medical associations wouldn't approve of their members moonlighting with magic.'

I snickered. Raven muttered something about witch 'doctors' being 'unprofessional' and shot me a sideways glance. 'It was a good idea, though.'

I grinned and took out my phone with renewed enthusiasm. 'All right. Now that we've got the witch's spell book in our possession, I'm going to contact the northern warlock.'

Aunt Ruth spun in her wheelchair. 'Great idea, but I can do that, Heather. I've had dealings with him before.'

I shook my head. 'I'll do it. It was me who broke the mirror, and I feel responsible for fixing it. I'll call him and explain the situation.'

'Very well.' Aunt Ruth smiled, but her eyes flashed a warning. 'Be aware that his manner can seem a bit unfriendly.' She paused for dramatic effect before adding in a low voice, 'And he can be a little forgetful.'

Raven narrowed his eyes sceptically. 'You mean he's unreliable?' he asked pointedly. 'Or untrustworthy?'

Aunt Ruth tilted her head. 'I wouldn't go that far. Anyway, he's the only warlock I know of who could fix my magic mirror.' She gave us both an impish smile. 'After all, he created it for me originally.'

'We'll have to trust that he'll do it,' I said with a sigh. 'We've no choice.'

Chapter 4

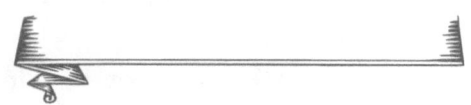

AUNT RUTH GAVE ME THE number, and I dutifully entered it into my phone. I took a deep breath before pressing the 'call' button, as a lump formed in my throat. I needed to make this work. Only a high-level witch or warlock could repair the magic mirror I'd broken, and Aunt Ruth needed it for her advanced magic, including, with luck, healing herself.

The phone rang several times before someone answered. By now, I was twisting my hair with one hand while Aunt Ruth and Raven watched expectantly, their faces tense.

'Abaddon Masana's residence. Zara speaking.'

I cleared my throat nervously and tried to be confident, despite how my voice quivered slightly. 'Hello, Zara,' I said in my best polite voice. 'I would like to speak to Abaddon, if possible.'

'He's busy,' Zara replied curtly, and I could visualise her reaching for the 'END CALL' button.

'Wait!' I practically shouted into the phone. 'Do you work for the warlock?'

'I assist him, yes,' Zara said with a sigh of impatience. 'What do you want?'

I ignored her rudeness and rushed on to explain our predicament. 'My aunt needs Abaddon's help. Her conduit and storage for magic is a large mirror, and it's been broken. She told me Abaddon could repair it.'

Zara huffed on the other end of the line. 'The earliest appointment is in six months.'

I groaned inwardly. 'We can't wait that long!' I said desperately, glancing over to where my aunt and Raven stared wide-eyed from across the room. I headed for the kitchen, so they wouldn't distract me. 'This is an emergency!'

A few seconds of silence passed before Zara spoke again. 'Hold on a moment,' she said in a clipped tone of voice that sounded suspiciously like someone trying to be polite without actually being polite at all. 'I'll get him.'

'I thought you said he's busy.'

'Yes. He's busy not answering the phone.'

Footsteps clattered on a tiled floor and faded to nothing after a few seconds. The line was silent for a minute, and I feared that Zara had hung up on me. But then she spoke again, her voice terse. 'I'll pass the phone over to him.'

'Abaddon Masana here. Who is this?' The warlock's voice sharpened at the edges, as if he was annoyed that I'd interrupted his important business.

I swallowed hard, introduced myself and quickly explained the dire situation to him of Aunt Ruth's condition and the damage to the magic mirror. I explained my aunt had obtained it from him originally. As I begged for his help, the desperation in my voice seeped through. Abaddon listened intently, but when I finished speaking, he did not respond immediately.

Finally, he sighed heavily. 'I will need some kind of payment for my services,' he said gruffly. 'A substantial one. Fixing a magic mirror like what you have described takes considerable time and energy, especially if it is of the magical quality I create.'

I hesitated for a moment. 'What might you want?'

'Something rare,' Abaddon replied with a meaningful smirk in his voice. 'Something that only powerful witches like your aunt would have.'

I grinned. 'I have the very thing—a witch's spell book full of information and spells. It's at least three hundred years old and is one of a kind.'

'Is that so?' His interest seemed piqued. 'And you will give me this book?' he asked, his tone softened.

'I will allow you to make a copy,' I replied. *I'm negotiating a great deal here. This is going to work!*

He harrumphed at my suggestion. 'Well, it won't be one of a kind then, will it?' Amusement coated his words.

'But it's still rare, and it's the content that is valuable, after all,' I said with a theatrical flourish of my hand, even though he couldn't see me in person.

'It is intriguing,' Abaddon admitted after a few moments of contemplation. 'I will help your aunt. Sometime this week or next is fine.'

His offer took me by surprise. 'Thank you for making space for my aunt. Your assistant told me you were busy and had no availability for six months.'

'Oh, I seldom see clients. Most of my time is taken up with personal research. I'd already blocked out the next six months for various projects. But, given your aunt's predicament and the compensation you offered, I will make an exception.'

'Awesome.' I did a mini fist pump. 'When can you come to Kingston upon Thames? Tomorrow? Or will you need a few days?'

I held my breath in anticipation, but Abaddon dashed my hopes. 'Oh, no, that's absolutely out of the question. I never make house calls. You'll have to come to my residence in Berwick upon Tweed.'

'Abaddon, my aunt can't travel right now, not so soon after her injury. The journey would be too demanding for her, and navigating the train stations and trains would be a nightmare, even with my assistance. Most of them aren't wheelchair friendly. Could you please reconsider?'

He remained unsympathetic. 'She doesn't need to come. You can bring the mirror by yourself.'

I shook my head firmly. 'No way! I don't want to leave her by herself overnight, let alone for any extended period. She's elderly, and has just suffered a terrible accident.' She did have Raven to look after her, and Pearl, her home help, came regularly, but they weren't family. I didn't trust them to care for my aunt the way I did.

The warlock sighed heavily, as if I were an annoying fly buzzing around his head he was desperate to swat away. 'This puts us at an impasse, then, my friend.'

'But... why don't you want to leave your house?' I asked, exasperated.

'Never mind why,' he snapped. 'I simply prefer to stay at home.'

Sighing in frustration, I resorted to pleading. 'Pretty please. Is there nothing I can say or do that will change your mind?'

'I told you I don't make house calls, Ms Nicholls,' Abaddon retorted with a sneer.

My heart sank, and my shoulders slumped. I frowned, racking my brain for another way to convince him. Abaddon was obviously reclusive, but I couldn't let my aunt suffer without the mirror's healing potential. I had no choice but to keep pushing.

'All I'm asking is you take the train from Berwick upon Tweed down here,' I begged. 'It will only take a few hours, and I'll meet you at the train station if you want. It'll make such a difference to my aunt's life.' *Short as it may be.*

'When you put it like that, it does sound like a decent thing to do,' he muttered grudgingly. 'Fine. I'll come tomorrow.'

I couldn't keep myself from grinning. 'Thank you so much, Abaddon. We truly appreciate this!'

'Yes, well, I should think so,' he grumbled. 'This is going to be an utter nuisance! Travelling is extremely inconvenient and uncomfortable, and the only thing worse than the stench of humanity it entails is their incessant conversation.'

After making the arrangements, I practically skipped back into the dining room to tell Aunt Ruth of my success. She clapped her hands with delight and praised me for being so determined.

MY PHONE RANG IN THE night's stillness, its insistent buzzing disturbing me from my bedtime reading. I picked it up and glanced at the caller ID. Rachel. Though it was late evening here in England, in New Zealand, it was already the following morning.

'Hey,' she said, her voice hushed with excitement. 'I know it's late there, but I had to tell you. I met someone at a professional meeting.'

Instinctively, my eyes widened with curiosity, and I perked up from the nearly dozing state I'd been in while reading. Rachel was a hard-working solicitor and rarely had time for socialising, but when she did, she could get wild. Her relationships were generally short-lived and far between because of her dedication to her work.

'Oh yeah? Tell me about him. I want to hear all the details,' I replied.

'He's a lawyer, obviously,' she said, 'but he works for a rival firm. He's tall and handsome and smart, like he stepped straight out of a Hollywood movie. He knows some of my acquaintances too. We hit it off at the conference and exchanged numbers, and he called a few days later and asked me out on a date! Can you believe it?'

'Sounds like a proper Prince Charming. What did you do on the date? What was he like? As nice as you hoped? What's his name?'

'Slow down with the questions. I'll get there. His name's Rick, and he's a real gentleman. He showed up on time with a bouquet of flowers and even opened the car door for me—I didn't know anyone did that anymore, did you?'

'No. Over here, if someone opens your car door, it might be to hijack the car.'

Rachel laughed. 'He took me to a teensy family-run Italian restaurant. It didn't look like much on the outside, but the food and the service were divine. Then he drove me up to the top of the Port Hills, and we gazed out over the city lights. We had such a cool evening together.'

'Woo... how romantic,' I said with a friendly sarcastic tease. 'What a sweet guy. I'm sure he's a real Adonis.'

Rachel sighed dreamily. 'He's gorgeous. And his lips are so luscious I could eat them.'

I rolled my eyes. 'Uh, huh. And what happened next?'

'Well... he drove me home after that. Then I...'

'You invited him in?'

'Kind of. It was more like I dragged him in behind me, you know?'

'You didn't!' I exclaimed, giggling. Oh yes. That sounded like my friend, all right.

'Oh, yeah,' she laughed. 'Things kind of escalated from there.'

I groaned. 'Please don't tell me it's X-rated already.'

'No, we just chatted for a while. He didn't try anything.'

'Oh.' How disappointing.

'So, I had to initiate things. Once I ripped his shirt open, he got the idea.'

'Rachel!' I laughed harder now. 'That's enough detail for me. But... was it fun?'

She gasped. 'It was... wow. The sex was mind blowing! Like nothing I'd ever experienced before. All through—'

I groaned again. 'Okay, Rachel! Stop right there. Please!' We weren't all getting laid at the moment. Raven, hottie as he was, couldn't stay in human form long enough for that.

'He's just... perfect, you know?'

Her voice and words echoed with awe, but with it came a tiny hint of scepticism.

'Too perfect?' I asked.

'Yeah, it looks that way. Flawless so far.'

'You've only just met. No one's perfect,' I said, my own scepticism coming out in my tone. 'But even if he is, do you want someone who's flawless in every way? Won't that be boring?'

'I don't know,' she admitted. 'He's a little too perfect. He's a senior partner in his firm. He seems rich, but is it all a façade? Maybe he has something to hide. Or maybe he's after my firm's clients.'

'Or trying to spy on your business? Have you got an important case?'

'Fuck. We have three important cases at the moment. One of them is mine. I didn't consider that.'

'Surely, no one would stoop so low as sleeping with someone to get inside information on a case.' *Except maybe reporters and lawyers. Hmm.*

'Maybe it is all for show. How can I be sure?' Rachel's fear and doubt were palpable.

'It's okay to be sceptical,' I said softly, 'and remember, it's okay to be cautious. There's no harm in getting to know him more and see how it goes.'

'Yeah,' she said, though she sounded far from convinced.

'Don't leave your confidential case notes lying around,' I reminded her. 'Take things with Rick one step at a time and see what happens. Maybe he is all you think he is.'

She sighed and agreed, though the doubt lingered in her voice. We said our goodbyes, and I hung up the phone, my head full of questions. Was this man really too good to be true? Could there be something more sinister beneath a façade of perfection? Was Rachel right to be wary, or was she merely letting her fears get the better of her?

If only I could have been there to support my friend in this.

Instead, I was on the other side of the world.

Chapter 5

THE NEXT MORNING, I made my way to work as usual, fingers crossed that Abaddon wouldn't show up before my shift was over. On the way, I stopped at the bakery and picked up a few almond croissants. And three chocolate eclairs for good measure. The poor baker was already sweating bullets from standing in front of those hot ovens since four in the morning. I dropped a few coins into her tip jar and wished her a good day.

At Chirtlewood, later in the morning, I encountered Maisey pacing back and forth in the small, windowless scullery. She didn't even look up when I entered. That was unusual for her.

'What's wrong, Maisey?' I whispered. I didn't want anyone to overhear me talking to a ghost.

She leaned back against one of the benches, like a spectre of smoke and shadows. I still didn't know how the ghosts could do things like that, acting as if they were solid flesh and blood, yet if I tried to touch one of them, they were as incorporeal as cold mist.

Maisey sighed in a way that only a ghost can sigh. 'Something wast stolen,' she bemoaned.

'The eggcups, yesterday. Yes, thanks, Maisey. I got them back. They're in their usual place in the kitchen.'

Maisey shifted her frail frame, her pale skin and measles spots illuminated by the shaft of light coming from the kitchen doorway. I forced myself not to recoil as she moved forward and thrust her ghostly, splotchy face too close for comfort.

'Nay, not those. The iron pestle is missing. Someone hath filched it from us!'

'The pestle?'

'Aye. See, thither afore me lies the mortar. Alas, the pestle hath gone.' She motioned to the space where a heavy pestle usually sat in a mortar, but it was no longer there.

Maisey was right. I searched, but it was nowhere to be found.

Why would someone steal an old pestle without the mortar? It made little sense. My mind wandered back to the blonde woman who had tried to nick our eggcups. She must have taken the pestle and left the mortar behind. But why?

The murmur of approaching visitors came from the kitchen, and Maisey vanished. I walked out to greet them, then gave them a tour of the large room, making especial mention of the cooking processes used four hundred years ago. Domestic history was one of my passions. I gestured at the enormous hearth and the hooks on either side of it that enabled giant spits and rods to be placed above a massive open fire underneath.

'There would have been a fire taking up most of that hearth,' I said. 'The cook could roast an entire pig on the spit over it, or simmer enough stew to feed a busy house, including the servants.' My gaze drifted to a cauldron in the corner. It always made me think of witchy things, rather than casserole.

'Wouldn't it be hot with an open fire of that size in here?' one woman asked.

'Absolutely. No air conditioning back then. The servants would sweat like crazy. But the aromas of the cooking food would be heavenly.'

WHEN I LEFT CHIRTLEWOOD later that day, Abaddon still had not made contact. Had he encountered problems on his journey? Maybe he'd made his own way from the train station and was waiting at home for me.

The late afternoon was overcast. The light rain from earlier had cleared away. I drove straight home, but Abaddon wasn't there. After greeting Aunt Ruth and Raven, I asked if they'd received any message from him.

'No,' Raven said. 'We've been home all day. He must still be on his way here.'

'That must be it, but I'm going to call him and find out what's up.'

I hit his number, and it kept ringing, but no one picked up.

We had no option now but to wait. A creeping thought that he hadn't left Berwick upon Tweed at all ran circles around my mind.

Raven stood. 'I'll cook dinner for us, and enough for the warlock if he's hungry when he arrives.'

'I'll help,' I said, getting up too. 'Maybe I can spice things up a little.'

Raven gave me a sideways look.

I giggled. 'I meant the food.'

Aunt Ruth smiled at us fondly. 'Thank you both,' she said. 'I really appreciate what both of you do.'

'It's no problem, Aunt Ruth,' I said over my shoulder as Raven strode ahead of me with a purposeful gait. I surveyed his muscular back, then allowed my gaze to drop to his taut backside. Nice. Those tight jeans were doing their job and then some!

I had to keep my hands off him at present, but that didn't stop me from admiring the view. Once the curse was broken—if it ever was—we could date properly. Until then, our relationship was purely platonic. Friends with postponed benefits.

Twenty minutes later, we ate a tasty meal of stir-fried chicken with lots of vegetables. Our conversation was subdued and the mood sombre, in contrast to last night.

Perhaps Abaddon had only pretended he was coming to put me off. He'd seemed like a rude person who would do that without a second thought. But if he didn't fix Aunt Ruth's magic mirror, what would we do?

I cleared away the plates. When I'd finished loading them into the dishwasher, I returned to the living room, where we continued to wait.

After another hour or so, someone knocked loudly on the front door.

Abaddon had arrived after all! Though why hadn't he called or texted or answered his phone?

The knocking came again. Two sharp raps.

'Coming, coming,' I called, scurrying to the front door.

I pulled it open with gusto. But it wasn't Abaddon there. A young girl of about seventeen or eighteen wearing a pointed green hat with long blonde hair cascading below it stood on the doormat. She wore a dark green jacket. Her boots and the bottom of her rolled-up jeans had spots of mud on them.

'It's about time,' she snapped and strode right into the house as if she owned it. 'I thought you'd never answer the door.'

I quickly checked outside to see if the warlock had accompanied her, but there was no sign of anyone else. 'Is Abaddon with you?' I asked hopefully.

The teenage girl spun on her heels on the wooden floor of the entrance hall with a flourish. 'He changed his mind and sent me instead.' She tossed her backpack onto the floor, and it hit the wall with a thud. She hung up her hat on the hooks by the door.

'You're Zara,' I said, still trying to take in this unexpected twist.

Zara flashed a lazy smile before her lips turned up into a smirk. 'Yes, I'm Zara,' she said mockingly. 'And I suppose you're Heather. You look older than you sounded on the phone.'

What a snarky girl. 'Did Abaddon tell you why he sent you here instead of coming himself?'

She shrugged and said nonchalantly, 'He said you needed someone to take care of a job pronto. That's all, and it's why I'm here. Though, honestly, I think he wanted to stay at home.' She gave me a sly smile before continuing. 'But enough about him. He's taught me enough nifty tricks to get the job done.'

Tricks? But only high-level witches and wizards had the spell-casting power to fix the magic mirror. And Zara was only a teenager. Was she powerful enough?

'Witchy magic comes into your family at a young age, does it?'

'Yes. Pre-teen.'

Aunt Ruth rolled into the hallway, her wheelchair gently pushed by Raven. Zara took a sharp intake of breath and shied away, as if startled.

'This is my Aunt Ruth and Raven,' I said, raising an eyebrow at Zara's jumpiness.

Zara swept one hand through her long blonde hair, struggling to compose herself again. 'I don't like it when people sneak up on me.'

'I don't sneak up on anyone,' Aunt Ruth replied coolly, her tone shaded with ice-cold disapproval. 'Especially in my own house.'

'Whatever.' Zara had shrunk back at Aunt Ruth's words, but quickly recovered and put on an air of nonchalance once again. 'Have you got any food?' she asked abruptly. 'I'm starving. Been riding buses and trains all bloody day.' She rolled her eyes dramatically.

'Come through into the dining room,' Raven said, motioning towards the door from which he and Aunt Ruth had entered. 'We've already eaten, but we cooked enough for... well, for whoever came.'

'Great. Thanks.' Zara followed Raven into the dining room.

Aunt Ruth gave me a meaningful look, her eyes glinting with curiosity. 'Do you think she can help us?' she mouthed.

'I don't know. This isn't quite what I expected. At all,' I replied quietly.

I went to the kitchen to prepare hot drinks for everyone while Zara dug into the meal Raven reheated for her. She didn't even bother thanking him for doing it.

We sat around the dining room table together, but Zara said little; in fact, she said almost nothing at all and didn't even lift her gaze from her plate as she devoured her meal. She must have been famished.

'Thank you for the cuppa,' Aunt Ruth said to me eventually, presumably to fill the void.

'No problem,' I said, taking a long swallow of my delicious white hot chocolate.

Zara took a swig of her tea and scrunched up her face as if she had swallowed something sour. 'This is the worst tea I've ever had.'

'What was the matter with it?' Raven sipped from his cup. 'It tasted perfectly fine to me.'

'It's weak, flavourless and tepid.' Zara pouted, folding her arms across her chest like a petulant child. 'If I gave the warlock a cup of tea like this, he'd—'

'He'd what?' I asked curiously, leaning forward slightly in my seat.

The girl shook her head like she had said nothing wrong, then mumbled, 'Never mind.'

I frowned. Zara was insufferable. How Abaddon could tolerate her attitude was beyond me, but maybe she didn't behave like this with him. Or maybe she was simply exhausted from her long journey.

Raven stood. 'Thanks for the drink, Heather,' he said pointedly before leaving the room. 'Good luck.' He said it as if he thought I might need more than luck if I was going to handle Zara and her mood swings.

Zara pushed her chair back from the table and wiped her mouth. 'So, I understand you have a magic mirror that needs to be repaired?'

Ah, so Abaddon *had* told her what the task was. But was Zara capable of carrying it out? She must be, seeing as the warlock had sent her in his place—or perhaps he wanted to get rid of her for a while. I couldn't blame him if he did.

Zara swivelled to face me with a glower. 'Abaddon told me you carelessly broke it.'

I was taken aback by her bluntness but nodded anyway. 'Yes,' I said hesitantly as a familiar pang of guilt hit me. 'Do you think you can fix it?'

'It depends on how badly it's damaged,' she replied matter-of-factly. 'Where is it?'

'In the spare room downstairs,' I said. 'I'll show you in a minute.' I got up and took Zara's plate to the kitchen. She hadn't appeared to be willing to do it herself.

When I came back, Zara had hoisted her backpack over one shoulder and was standing by the door to the hall. 'Lead the way,' she commanded with a wave of her hand.

Aunt Ruth's sprawling house was vast. Many of the rooms were shut off, with Aunt Ruth never once telling me what was hidden away behind the locked doors. But she had shown me the downstairs guest room. It was two doors along from the room she'd taken as her bedroom following her accident. I took Zara there, my soft-soled shoes making little sound on the wooden floorboards, a sharp contrast to Zara's clonking boots.

We went inside. I had propped the mirror frame up against the far wall next to the window.

Zara dropped her backpack on the bed. She stepped nearer and studied the intricate carvings on its frame. She ran her fingers delicately over them like she was tracing the lines on an ancient map.

'Where's the glass?' she asked without shifting her gaze.

My cheeks grew hot as I cleared my throat nervously. 'Gone.' I replied, sheepishly glancing away. 'I sorta threw it out... Can you fix it?' I repeated with a lump in my throat.

Zara didn't turn around. 'I think so.'

'You're not sure?'

'It might be beyond my magical capabilities.'

My nostrils flared and my eyes narrowed. I moved in front of her, forcing her to face me. 'And what about Abaddon? Why didn't he come like he promised? Can he repair it?'

'The whims of warlocks are not for me to question.'

Was there a trace of fear in her face and a slight tremble in her voice? 'All right. Let's talk about this tomorrow. You must be exhausted from your trip. Do you have a place to stay?' I asked.

Zara sat on the bed and kicked off her muddy boots before turning her attention to the room. 'This will do,' she said with a resigned sigh. 'It's certainly not five stars, but it could be worse.' She yawned.

My first instinct was to reply with something rude myself, but I quickly reconsidered. I needed Zara's cooperation, if only to help convince Abaddon to come himself. It would be easier if she stayed here.

'See you in the morning if you're up before I leave,' I said, forcing a smile. 'I have to go to work early.'

Zara was already sprawled on the bed, one arm over her eyes, when I pulled the door closed behind me.

Chapter 6

EARLY NEXT MORNING, I prepared breakfast in bed for Aunt Ruth and shared a coffee and a few laughs with Raven. When he got up to put away his breakfast things, I opened my phone to check my emails.

Rachel had sent me one, but from her work email address, not her personal one. She was handling everything to do with my legal separation from that bastard Terry. This communication must be something to do with that.

Raven sat again. 'What's wrong?' he asked. 'You're frowning.'

'It's an email from my lawyer,' I replied, opening it and scanning it quickly. A flood of relief swept through me. 'It's good news. The house sale is finally confirmed! I'll get some money from that—though it won't be much once the mortgage is paid off. The best thing is that I won't have any assets shared with Terry after this.'

'That's quick. You only put it on the market a few weeks ago, didn't you?'

'Yes. It's not any quicker than usual. If anything, it took longer.'

Raven shook his head. 'It takes months here for a house sale to go through, and it can still fail at the last minute.'

'That sounds stressful.'

He nodded. 'Yeah.'

I left for Chirtlewood a few minutes later. Zara hadn't emerged from the guest room before I went. I hadn't wanted to leave my aunt and Raven to face her without me, but we were short-staffed at the manor. Lydia, Penny and I were working six or seven days a week to manage the house and its visitors. I couldn't leave the pair of them to do it alone unless absolutely necessary. Zara would have to wait.

Who was I kidding? By the time I got home after work, Aunt Ruth would have sorted everything out. The girl could surely do something, otherwise Abaddon wouldn't have sent her. And Raven would back up Aunt Ruth if Zara wasn't forthcoming.

I bid goodbye to them both, headed out and drove to work.

In the staff office at Chirtlewood House, Lydia smiled as she served the delicious cinnamon swirls to Penny and me. 'Two each, I think!'

'So tasty,' Penny said, licking her lips eagerly.

I said with dread in my voice for the upcoming battle with my waistline, 'I'd better go up and down the stairs twenty times today to try to work off some of that pastry. Otherwise, all the progress I've made since my operation is going right out the window!'

Lydia nodded knowingly. 'You've done great, just like I said you would. But we need these treats with all the running around we do all day. Come on—let's eat!'

The morning was busy, and I quickly lost count of the number of times I climbed the grand staircase to check on visitors to the house looking around upstairs. When I'd first started at Chirtlewood, about a month ago, I'd had to stop on the landing halfway to catch my breath, but thankfully I didn't have to do that anymore. I could climb those stairs like a gazelle. A slightly overweight gazelle with a bad knee, anyway.

At lunch, I sat alone in the office, eating my tuna and Norwegian cheese sandwich and scrolling through my phone. A newspaper lying on the table—the local *Surrey Comet*—caught my attention out of the corner of my eye. Or, rather, the headline did: 'Body of woman pulled from river.' What the hell?

I drew the newspaper closer and read the first few paragraphs. A passer-by had spotted a body floating in the Thames near Richmond during the night, caught up in rushes at the riverbank. She had drowned several hours earlier, apparently, and the police were investigating the circumstances of the death.

A photo of the dead woman graced the front page to the right of the article itself. A middle-aged, blonde woman. I scrutinised the photo, sure I'd seen that face before.

I gasped. It was the woman I'd caught trying to steal the eggcups two days ago!

Eyes wide, I raced through the rest of the report. Her name was Jane Middlemore. Divorced, lived alone, one child. Police were searching for witnesses. The article stated that anyone with information about the woman and her recent movements should inform the police immediately.

I was still intently studying the newspaper when Lydia came in. That was my cue to get back to work, but I had to show her this. As she unwrapped her lunch, I pushed the newspaper across the table to her. 'Have a look. That's the woman who tried to pinch our eggcups.'

Lydia leaned in for a closer look at the photo. 'So it is. What a coincidence!'

'I better get back out there and keep an eye on things,' I said.

'Let's chat about this later. We might have to let the police know that she was here only two days ago.'

I left the office and did a quick reconnaissance of the ground floor. I didn't find Penny, so I assumed she was upstairs. There were two groups of visitors wandering around, whispering excitedly to each other and snapping photos of the portraits and the grand staircase. They had guidebooks and didn't appear to want to ask questions, so I left them to it and continued my patrol.

Lydia approached me in the afternoon during a quiet spell. 'Heather, I think we might have to contact the police about this woman thief business,' she said with an agitated sigh. 'They want to know about her movements in the last few days, and seeing as she tried to steal from us, it could be important information. Though I don't understand how, personally.'

I was already leaning towards the same conclusion. 'Fine. Let's go to the police station together after work.'

Two hours later, Lydia and I sauntered up to the reception at the Kingston police station and asked to speak with Detective Inspector Pentecost.

A constable who appeared barely any older than my daughter showed us into her office. The inspector was tall and smartly dressed. She raised her eyebrows as soon as we entered.

'We're not here about the murder at Chirtlewood,' Lydia said quickly, referring to the tragedy of the previous month.

'Then why are you here?' she asked.

'Because the woman who was found in the river visited Chirtlewood the day before yesterday,' Lydia said.

'Ms Middlemore.' The inspector gestured to two chairs. 'Please, take a seat and tell me about her visit.'

We sat, and I started to explain. 'I stopped her at the exit because I was suspicious that she might have something in her bag that belonged to the manor, as her bag looked fuller than when she had arrived. It turned out she'd taken some items from the kitchens and was trying to smuggle them out.'

'Were they valuable?' the inspector asked, leaning forward on her elbows.

I turned to Lydia. She shrugged and said, 'Not particularly. It was a pair of eggcups.'

'Eggcups?' Inspector Pentecost's forehead creased in consternation. 'Why would she want those?'

I raised my hands in a futile attempt to explain her motives. 'For boiled eggs, maybe?' I suggested. 'There was something else,' I said. 'We—I discovered this morning that a pestle is missing from the kitchen.'

Now Lydia turned to me. 'Wait a minute—you never mentioned that earlier!'

'I didn't have a chance at the time, and then I got side-tracked.' I shrugged apologetically.

'Can I clarify that?' the inspector said. 'Do you mean a pestle as in a pestle and mortar?'

'That's right, but she only took the pestle. I'm guessing it was her, anyway, although I didn't see it in her bag. Maybe it was in a pocket.'

'How odd.'

Something about the inspector's tone of voice and manner seemed a little 'off'. Her tone was flat, even disinterested. Or unsurprised about this behaviour from the late Ms Middlemore.

'What do you know about her?' I asked. 'Was she a minor thief? A thief of minor items? Maybe she had a compulsion to steal?'

'A kleptomaniac,' Lydia added.

Inspector Pentecost angled her head, her demeanour nonchalant but her eyes sharp. 'You must realise I can't tell you that. But thank you for the information you provided. It's interesting background.'

'So, she was a compulsive thief, wasn't she?' I said.

The inspector folded her arms, her lips pursed in disapproval. 'I didn't say that.'

'We're intuitive.' Lydia smiled.

The inspector slowly unfolded her arms and let out an exasperated sigh. 'I'll show you out.'

Lydia and I exchanged glances. 'There's no need. We know the way.'

Once outside, Lydia elbowed me in the ribs to get my attention. 'I think we should look into this ourselves, Heather. You know, investigate.'

We? Where did this come from? 'Investigate what, exactly? And how?'

Lydia said nothing more until we'd got to our cars. We paused there, and she finally spoke, her voice low and conspiratorial. 'There's a mystery here, Heather. The police are investigating her death. That means they don't know whether it's suicide, an accident or maybe even murder.'

'You don't think it's got anything to do with Chirtlewood, do you?' I eyed her sceptically.

'No,' she answered quickly. 'That woman probably stole from everywhere. I'm sure it was only coincidence that she targeted Chirtlewood the day before she died. But don't you see? It brought her to our attention, into our sphere of contact, in a way. We owe it to her to investigate. You, me and the ghosts. Like you did with the murder last month.' Lydia's voice rose and she gestured wildly as she spoke. She was obviously excited by this.

I considered it for a moment. After I'd solved a mystery myself last month, Lydia now wanted to get in on the act. And I was as keen as she was to uncover the truth because of my burning curiosity. Besides, we could make it another outing with the manor ghosts.

'You're on,' I said and offered my fist for a bump. 'Tomorrow after work, let's get started.'

She completed the fist bump. 'Not tonight?'

I grinned at her eagerness. 'Sorry. I've got something important I have to do at home. Besides, shouldn't we come up with a plan first?'

Lydia nodded thoughtfully. 'That sounds sensible. How about we meet at Chirtlewood half an hour early tomorrow and talk through some ideas?'

'Sounds like a good suggestion,' I said as I opened the car door. 'See you then.'

Chapter 7

I ARRIVED HOME LATER than usual because of my trip to the police station. Everyone else had already eaten, but Raven reheated the dinner he'd saved for me in the microwave. I gave him a broad smile and a peck on the cheek when he handed me the plate of shepherd's pie, or as he liked to call it, Raven's pie.

He trembled as his cheeks turned a light shade of pink.

'Stay human!' I said, half joking, half serious.

Raven bit his bottom lip. 'Are you teasing me?'

'Only a little.' I headed towards the dining room. 'I want a proper date once you can handle a bit of flirting without turning into a bird.'

'Heather, I—'

The blinding flash of light caused stars to flash before my eyes, and I almost dropped the plate. When my vision cleared, Raven had already changed into his bird form and was escaping through the window into the twilight.

'Oh, shit,' I grumbled.

Aunt Ruth wheeled into the kitchen, shaking her head at me. 'Not again. Will you stop harassing the poor man? What did you say this time?'

'I honestly don't know what triggered the curse. I was being perfectly platonic.'

She rolled her eyes towards the ceiling as if seeking divine answers. 'It must have been his vivid imagination, then.'

'I'm only trying to help him get used to me being around him.'

'I know. Go eat your dinner before it gets cold again.'

I did as I was told. Aunt Ruth kept me company while I ate and regaled me with tales of her adventures. Her home help, Pearl, had taken her out for a walk and to a café, besides completing several household chores. My gratitude to Pearl knew no bounds.

I told Aunt Ruth about the woman who'd drowned in the river and how Lydia and I intended to investigate with the help of Chirtlewood's ghosts.

'Really? That ploy worked out so well last time, didn't it? You almost got fired.'

'Don't worry. That won't happen this time. Lydia's my boss, remember? What could possibly go wrong?'

Aunt Ruth arched an eyebrow at me. 'Oh, right. Well, try not to get into too much trouble.'

'I won't,' I promised before getting up and taking my plate back to the kitchen. I slotted it into the dishwasher and returned to the dining room. 'How about we talk to Zara and sort out what's going to happen with your mirror and the witch's spell book?'

'Good idea. She was in the living room, the last I saw her.'

We made our way there and found Zara lying full length on the sofa with three empty crisp packets on the floor beside her. The television displayed a music reality show. She gave us a disinterested glance before switching the television to mute and giving us her languid attention.

'Hello, Zara,' I said cheerfully. 'Have you determined if you can fix the magic mirror without Abaddon's help?'

'Yes,' she replied. Her gaze shifted sideways.

'You can do it, then?' I asked hopefully.

Zara shook her head and fixed me with a baleful glare that could have withered a flower on contact. 'No,' she said flatly, 'I can't.'

I sighed heavily. 'Did you get a chance to speak to the warlock himself?'

Zara pushed herself up with a resolute expression. 'No, I didn't. But I'm sure he'll want me to take the mirror home to Berwick upon Tweed. He'll fix it there. And I'll have to take the witch's spell book with me too. He'll copy that. I'll bring them back here afterwards.'

'Well, if that's the only way—'

'Get off your broomstick!' Aunt Ruth snapped. 'It sounds like a terrible idea to me. Abaddon himself told Heather that he's very busy. What guarantee do we have that he'll repair the mirror straight away, or even at all? Once he's copied the witch's spell book, he'll probably spend all his time poring through it, if I know him, rather than fixing the mirror.'

Zara cocked her head and shot Aunt Ruth a suspicious glance. 'Do you know him?'

'Not particularly well, but enough to know he'll be much more interested in studying the spell book than carrying out magical repair work.'

I blinked and shook my head in confusion. 'Wait a minute,' I said. 'I don't understand this, Zara. I understood you were going to copy the witch's spell book as Abaddon's payment for repairing the mirror. You said you can't fix the mirror, but now you're saying you can't copy the spell book either? What gives?'

'Um... that's right,' she replied sheepishly, gripping the edge of her seat with both hands as if anticipating an interrogation.

'Why not?' I asked, perplexed.

She leapt up with a strangled cry, her cheeks already wet with tears. 'It's not my fault! The warlock gave me a scroll with a spell on it to copy the spell book, but I wanted to practise it first. I didn't want to make a mistake with the real thing, so I used a paperback I picked up at the bus station and tried it out on that.'

'Did it work?' I asked, only half expecting it had.

'Yeah... It worked great.' Zara's eyes widened, as if stunned by her own success. Then her mouth turned down into a frown.

'So... what's the problem?'

'The spell was wiped clean off the scroll after I used it. And I can't remember all of it!' Zara wailed. 'He's going to—'

'Bewitched and bedevilled idiocy!' Aunt Ruth muttered. 'Didn't Abaddon tell you it was a single-use spell scroll?'

The girl shrugged and let out a sob.

I moved to her side and wrapped an arm around her shoulders to offer some comfort. 'Try not to be upset. It's done now. There's still plenty of time for us to put things right.' I turned to Aunt Ruth. 'Are you sure we shouldn't send the spell book and mirror with Zara to Abaddon? We can ask if he'll make it a priority.'

'Absolutely not.' Aunt Ruth's jaw set in a hardened line. She wouldn't change her mind on this.

It was pointless to argue. But what was the solution? I didn't want to leave Aunt Ruth. Would Raven go? No, it wouldn't be fair to him. Besides, I couldn't ask him anyway because he'd flown off into the night.

'Zara, are you worried about speaking to Abaddon about this?' I asked, trying to keep my voice light despite the horrible tension in the room. 'Do you think he'll be angry? You said, "He's going to—" something. What is he going to do?'

Zara sat again, her lower lip trembling. 'Never mind.'

'Does he bully you, Zara?' Aunt Ruth asked, her tone expressing concern.

The poor girl buried her face in her hands and mumbled something indistinguishable.

I sighed and stood up, my mind already formulating another plan. 'Aunt Ruth, I think we'd better keep Zara here for the time being. I'll call the warlock and insist he come down here himself. He might get angry, but he can get angry at me instead, not at Zara. I can handle it.'

Aunt Ruth nodded sagely and added, 'It's all because of his own doing, anyway. If he had come like he said he would, we wouldn't be in this situation now.'

A SPELL OF MIRROR MAGIC

AUNT RUTH AND I RETURNED to the kitchen, leaving Zara in the living room. I made white hot chocolates for myself and Aunt Ruth with extra sugar and marshmallows on the side. We deserved it after Zara's admission, which had left us crestfallen.

When I put the mugs on the kitchen table, Aunt Ruth said, 'This isn't working out the way I expected it to.'

'I'll call the warlock,' I said determinedly. 'Once I explain the situation to him, I'm sure he'll understand and be more willing to help.'

Aunt Ruth snorted and shook her head. 'Don't count on it. I'm not sure I trust him at all now.'

'Why? Because he didn't come himself? Sure, he said he would, but maybe his agoraphobia got the better of him, so he sent his assistant.'

Aunt Ruth narrowed her eyes. 'Perhaps he never intended to come himself at all. Maybe he sent Zara to steal the witch's spell book, and all this drama of hers is an act to put us off our guard.'

'Oh, come on, Aunt Ruth,' I said with a laugh. 'Surely not. That sounds unlikely. He would ruin his reputation if he did that.'

'You never know,' she replied wistfully, tapping her fingers against the edge of the table. 'Why send her if she couldn't do anything to help?'

My aunt had forgotten about the spell scroll that Zara had used up. Or maybe she didn't believe there had been a spell scroll at all. I sipped at my drink while I collected my thoughts. 'Maybe Abaddon truly thought she could repair the magic mirror. And she explained that she accidentally wiped the scroll to copy the spell book. It's not her fault.'

Aunt Ruth shrugged her shoulders with an expression of disbelief on her face. 'It all seems too convenient to me. If you haven't noticed, I put the witch's spell book on the shelf with our cooking books—she'll never find it there. It's probably sensible to be cautious.'

'I'll call Abaddon now.' I hit his number on my phone. Would he answer the call himself, or would he ignore it because his assistant was away?

It rang and rang, and I was about to give up when he finally answered. 'Abaddon Masana here. Who is this, and what do you want?'

His irate telephone manner jolted me. Had I woken him up from a nap or pulled him away from his dinner? 'It's Heather Nicholls. I'm calling about the work you agreed to do for me.'

'Oh, yes. I sent Zara. Has she not turned up yet?'

'She's here, but she's not able to perform the spells herself.'

'Is that so?' He sounded dubious. 'What seems to be the problem?'

'She says she's unable to complete the work because her magic isn't powerful enough.' I rubbed my forehead with one hand. 'She accidentally wiped the scroll to copy the witch's spell book, and now we need you to come and help.'

'Well, that's unfortunate. I'm afraid there's nothing more I can do.'

'But you told us you were coming yourself!' I gripped my phone so tightly my fingers hurt. Even though it wasn't Abaddon's fault, he'd deceived us, and now he didn't intend to fix the situation himself.

'Did I? Maybe I did. But I believed Zara would help you.'

He sounded sincere and even genuinely regretful. 'Do you think you could come here yourself and sort this problem out?'

Abaddon sighed deeply into the phone—a sound that might almost have been sympathy—before replying. 'I'm afraid I'm busy with another matter at the moment. But if you offer enough of an incentive, I could be persuaded to fit you in.'

'Thank you. We can discuss extra payment when you arrive.' I needed to get him here. I'd worry about the payment later.

He paused, as if considering this for a few moments. 'Very well. I'll be there tomorrow evening. But please understand, this is most unusual. I seldom leave my home for anything, so the fee must be worth my while.' He hung up without waiting for me to respond.

Aunt Ruth took my hand in hers. 'At least he says he's coming. We'll simply have to wait and see if he actually does it.'

I nodded. 'And hope he doesn't set too high a price.'

THE INCESSANT RINGING of the phone shattered the peace of the night. I squinted at the time on its vibrating face: 3.17 am. Rose was video calling me.

I thrust my legs over the side of the bed and sat up so fast my head spun. This could be an emergency—or maybe she was calling for some middle-of-the-night chit-chat. She sometimes forgot I wasn't living in the same time zone as her anymore.

I picked up the phone with a groan. 'Hello?' I said sleepily.

'Mum, it's me.' Rose's grimacing face appeared on the screen.

My stomach churned. 'Rose. What's wrong?'

'I just had a phone call from Dad, and I'm furious!'

This can't be good...

I was wide awake now and ready to battle any dragons that threatened my daughter's well-being. But I had to remain composed. 'Take a deep breath, sweetheart, and tell me what happened.'

Rose inhaled and exhaled deeply, her breathing coming through her phone so loud I imagined it brushing my face.

'Dad told me you've got a definite buyer for the house,' she said. 'Is that right?'

'Yes. Rachel says the sale will go through in a few days.' Rachel was my lawyer and my best friend. 'But why are you so upset?' I paused for a moment before continuing. 'I put everything of yours into storage. The house is empty now, but your stuff is safe.'

'That's not it—Dad told me he wants to move to Wellington and crash at my place until he sorts his shit out,' Rose said, her voice frantic.

'If Terry's going to stay with you until he sorts his shit out, he'll be there for months, if not years.' Maybe for the rest of his life.

'I know! That's what I mean. It'll be too much. I'm only sharing a small flat with other students. There's nowhere for him to sleep except on the floor in my room. And then I'll have no privacy.' Rose was almost hysterical now, her voice rising to a shrill pitch.

'Tell him no, then.'

'You know what he's like, Mum. He'll simply turn up on the doorstep and insist.'

Yeah, he would. I was legally separated from Terry and living on the other side of the world, but he still found ways to mess with my life and cause chaos. Now he was setting his sights on our daughter.

'Let's back up a bit,' I said. 'Did your dad tell you why he's moving to Wellington?'

'He told me he's going to use his share of the money from the house sale to start a management consultancy business up here.' Rose rolled her eyes, exasperation clear in her words.

'Oh, so now he's going to get a bloody job, is he? If he's going to be working, why can't he rent or buy a place instead of moving in with you?'

'He said some stuff about conserving capital and whatnot. He was so vague I don't think even he knew what the fuck he was talking about.'

'Yeah, that might be the case.' I paused. Rose had calmed down. 'Do you want me to step in and try to talk some sense into him, or do you want to handle it yourself?'

'I've got this, Mum. I can handle him. It's just that when he called me a few minutes ago, he surprised me with his sense of entitlement—the idea that he could simply move in and take over my space because he wanted to without even asking me. I only have one room in a shared flat. He didn't listen when I told him that.'

'I know exactly what you mean, Rose.' I'd had twenty years of that experience myself. 'Use the broken record technique: say the same thing over and over until it finally goes into his block head. You're not responsible for housing him. He can afford to do that himself after the house sale going through.'

'Okay. Thanks. I feel better simply talking to you about it, Mum.' Rose sighed in relief, as if our chat had lifted a weight from her shoulders.

'That's what mothers are for.' I allowed myself a satisfied smile.

Rose gasped. 'Oops, I just saw the time! Sorry, it's the middle of the night for you. Did I wake you up?'

'Yes, but never mind.' I sighed. 'I want you to know that when you need me, I'm here for you.'

'Thanks for being so understanding,' Rose said gratefully. 'I'll let you get back to sleep now. Night, night, Mum.'

She smiled and disconnected.

Chapter 8

I ARRIVED AT WORK EARLY to meet Lydia and work out a plan for investigating Jane Middlemore's death. Questions swirled around my mind as I banged through the office door, a bag of croissants in my arms. What compelled Jane to steal trivial items, including from Chirtlewood? Was her death accidental—or not? Was it connected to her petty thefts? It seemed unlikely.

I put the croissants on the table. Lydia arrived a few moments later.

'How are you this morning, Heather?' she asked.

'I'm good. Except my knee is sore again. I think I strained it on my last walk, somehow.'

'You have a sore knee? You haven't mentioned that before.'

'It's a tennis injury from when I was a teenager.'

Lydia glanced at the croissants hungrily. 'I thought that was supposed to be elbows.'

'Yeah, funny. Not. I twisted my knee in a fall. It never healed properly. Sometimes, the pain comes back. Panadeine works, though. How are you?'

Lydia groaned. 'My hip aches again. It's a bloody nuisance. I'll stay downstairs as much as possible today. I'll see if Penny is happy to work upstairs all day so we can give our hips and knees a rest from the grand staircase.'

'Okay. So... how about we discuss how we're going to investigate Jane Middlemore's drowning? Any ideas?'

'Let's see if any of the ghosts are around, so we can ask for their help,' she suggested. 'The more of us there are, the easier it will be to find Jane's ghost, if it is still in the area.'

'Countess Chirtle?' I called as we walked into the entrance hall. Sometimes she appeared when I called her name. 'Charlotte?'

A gust of chilled air whirled around us. We shivered.

After a few moments, she materialised on the grand staircase with a dramatic flair, swirling ethereal gown and all. She descended to the tiled entrance hall, her long, dark hair cascading around her.

'Good day, Heather and Lydia. Hast you something to inquire of me?'

I nodded. 'Yes, we do. Lydia and I would like to investigate the death of a local woman called Jane Middlemore. She drowned in the river a few nights ago.'

Charlotte hummed sympathetically and contemplated us thoughtfully before answering. 'Oh, how truly wretched! Pray tell, how might I be of service to thee?'

'We were wondering if you or any of the other ghosts could discover anything that might help us work out what happened to her,' I said.

Charlotte considered this for a moment before nodding. 'Verily, when a life is cut short in such a tragic fashion, the unfortunate one's broken soul oft dwells in the vicinity of their demise, wandering in search of a modicum of understanding as to wherefore they wast torn from this life so suddenly.' She paused and added, 'My fellow phantoms of Chirtlewood and I art most able to bring some understanding to light about this macabre puzzle.'

'Thank you, Charlotte. It's great that you will help us. Shall we all go to the river after Chirtlewood closes today in search of Jane's ghost? Could it still be there after this time?'

'Perchance, if the lady is resolute in her desire to tread this world forever. Elsewise, nigh certes she hath left this corporeal realm.'

'But how likely is it that we will find her?' Lydia asked.

'The world isn't crowded with ghosts,' I said. 'It seems to be quite rare when they remain after death.'

We both waited for Charlotte to provide answers.

'Verily, 'tis so. Apparitions art as rare as eggs from a golden goose.'

'Dammit,' Lydia said. 'Well, we must at least go and search in case she's still around. Her apparition, I mean.'

'Oh, aye. A jaunt. We wilt certes plan for such a thing. I shalt converse with the earl and Maisey. I am sure they shalt be as enthusiastic as I am at the prospect of this outing!'

'That's great,' Lydia said with a relieved sigh. 'Thank you.'

Footsteps trod toward us, and we whirled around. Penny emerged into the entrance hall, her eyes narrowed in suspicion. 'I heard voices. Is something going on I should know about?'

Penny wasn't a trainee witch like Lydia and I were and couldn't interact with the ghosts, though she knew the house was haunted.

'No, nothing,' Lydia said, her expression strained. 'We both arrived a little early. I was only thanking Heather for bringing the pastries today.'

Penny quirked an eyebrow and crossed her arms over her chest suspiciously. 'In here? You're both facing the stairs like you were talking to someone else. Did you think you heard a ghost or something?' She chuckled, apparently trying to make light of the circumstances.

Lydia's gaze shifted downwards. 'It must have been. There's no one else here. Let's go eat those croissants and then get the house opened up for visitors.' With that, she grabbed my arm, and we swept past Penny, her pale face still bearing an expression of uncertainty.

I tried my best to keep a straight face as Lydia led us away.

THE DAY AT CHIRTLEWOOD moved at a glacial pace. I meandered down the hallways and through the rooms, tirelessly waiting for the end of the day when we could set out on our mission to find Jane's ghost—if it remained earthbound.

From time to time, I stared out the windows towards the trees lining the riverbank in the distance, knots forming in my stomach. *Where, oh where, is Raven, and is he safe?*

Finally, the time arrived when we could politely ask the remaining visitors to make their way out because the manor house was about to close. Once they'd all gone, we locked up the front entrance. Penny prepared to head out as well. Lydia muttered something about the bookkeeping she still had to do, while I mumbled something about needing to use the bathroom before leaving. Penny had no idea Lydia and I were about to embark on an adventure with the manor ghosts accompanying us. We watched her drive off.

Charlotte had been waiting at the bottom of the grand staircase until Lydia and I were on our own. 'Wilt we tarry longer?' she asked.

'I think we're ready,' I said. 'How about we walk along the riverbank? It's nice out.' I wouldn't have time for my usual walk in Richmond Park after this mission.

The countess shrugged. 'It makes no difference to us.'

'A walk would be marvellous,' Lydia agreed.

She unlocked the front door to let us through, then locked it again behind us. At the bottom of the front steps, all the ghosts waited: the countess, whose eyes twinkled with anticipation; the earl, sitting in a ghostly wheelchair because he couldn't walk far, even in ghostly form; the earl's spectral border collie, Scruffles, whose tail wagged in time with each ghostly woof; and Maisey, who skipped around joyfully at the prospect of a grand new adventure.

We set off across Chirtlewood's expansive gardens, which were bursting with vibrant colours—vivid greens, pinks, purples and yellows all combining to create a breath-taking landscape amidst towering trees offering dappled shade. In the fresh air, the sweetness of jasmine and roses reached my nose in a heavenly mix.

The wrought-iron gates led us to the pathway alongside the river, shimmering in the late afternoon sun. Numerous couples and individuals with their dogs strolled along. Scruffles took great delight in alarming the other canines and their owners with his spooky barking, because they could not determine where it came from. Maisey scrambled after Scruffles, desperately trying to keep him reined in as he caused chaos everywhere he went.

The countess sauntered along beside us, pushing the earl in his wheelchair with relative ease.

The earl was in his usual cantankerous mood. 'I'm only coming along for the walk,' he declared. 'Verily, 'tis an aim of most wondrous futility, and thou art doomed to fail abysmally in its accomplishment. I am confident this foray shalt be a complete waste of our hours.'

'Thanks for that,' I muttered, putting as much sarcasm in my voice as I could muster.

'Might not but thee be so disagreeable?' Charlotte said. 'Oh, how rare 'tis for us to hast intent in our days. Allow us to make this excursion a pleasant one, regardless of the ensuing outcome.'

'Nay need for that tone,' the earl grumbled. 'I wast merely expressing mine opinion.'

'If I hath said something disagreeable to me parents,' Maisey said, 'I would hast been made to do the heaviest chores of all yond day.'

'Bah! That is but a mere trifle of a punishment,' the earl snapped. ''Tis far simpler and more expeditious to chastise a dissenting miscreant with a flogging.'

I gasped. 'Nowadays, we don't flog people for their opinions.'

'Naturally, I include not mine own self,' the earl declared. 'As an earl, I deemed it only fitting to bestow upon a loyal servant the grim burden to be punished in my stead when I wast a boy.'

'The origin of the expression "a whipping boy",' Lydia said, almost as if she had been waiting for me to ask.

'No way!' I said, my eyes wide with surprise.

Lydia nodded solemnly. 'For royalty, yes. It was the convention for some of the more powerful families in Europe.' She lowered her voice. 'The earl obviously thought the same applied to him.'

We continued along the riverbank and entered Richmond. On our left, the river meandered slowly along. On our right, local cafes were alive with laughter and chatter, their inviting scents of coffee and baked goods tantalising us as we passed. Most other shops had already closed for the day.

Maisey and Scruffles ran on far ahead, out of sight.

Unfortunately, the ghost of Jane Middlemore was nowhere to be found.

We came to a stop most of the way through Richmond village. I glanced at the earl, expecting a smug 'I told you so' quip, but it didn't come—though his expression was more than a little dour. Perhaps he would have rather stayed at home.

'Verily, if the wretched woman's spirit tarried, 'tis gone now,' Charlotte said. 'Unless 'tis yond Maisey hath already encountered the lady in her explorations. Ah, thither she comes back with Scruffles in tow.'

Maisey came into view at impressive speed, the furry bundle of energy that was Scruffles bounding along at her feet. Had she found the ghost of the drowned woman and was hurrying to tell us the news? My hopes were soon dashed. Maisey wasn't trying to get our attention—she was merely enjoying the outing.

She pulled up next to us, panting. 'We ventured several furlongs forth,' Maisey gasped, 'yet nary an inkling of the poor lady's apparition wast to be made out.'

'Thank you for your effort, Maisey,' I said. 'We had to try.'

Lydia scrunched up her face and sighed. 'What shall we do next? Is our investigation at a dead end already?'

I wracked my brains, trying to think of the best way forward. 'We need to learn more about Jane Middlemore, dig deeper into her life. Perhaps we can talk to her family or neighbours—anyone who knew her well. I'm sure they'll have plenty of stories and anecdotes that will shed light on her life and death.'

Charlotte nodded. 'Aye, 'tis a splendid bethought. Let us wend thither and hold discourse forthwith.'

'I'm keen,' Lydia said, 'but it's getting a bit late. Can we do this tomorrow?'

'Yes, great idea,' I agreed. 'I can't do any more this evening either. I have something urgent to do for my aunt.'

'In the meantime, I'll find out where Jane lived,' Lydia offered.

'Very well,' Charlotte agreed. 'Allow us to continue with this task on the morrow come evenfall. Now we ought to return to the manor.'

We went back the way we had come. The early evening had become a little cooler, but the stroll was as pleasant as before.

I tried to focus on the riverside walk rather than on the hurricane of thoughts swirling through my mind. Was I taking on too much? Perhaps I should leave this to Charlotte, her ghostly companions and Lydia, while I concentrated on getting Aunt Ruth's mirror fixed.

That made sense, but finding out what had happened to Jane Middlemore was important to me. It was as if her being at Chirtlewood the day before her death, and drawing attention to herself, was like a sign. One I couldn't ignore. She was a witch, like Lydia and I. In some small way, that gave us a connection.

Besides, who said a little adventure couldn't be fun? A little mystery and mayhem never killed anyone... not me, anyway. Not yet.

Chapter 9

I RUSHED HOME, STILL puzzling over Jane Middlemore's untimely death. The warlock said he would arrive tonight, and I didn't want to be away from home when he got there. Dammit. I could do two things at once with ease most of the time, but I couldn't be in two places at once.

At home, I gave Aunt Ruth a hug and asked her about her day. She'd been out with Pearl, who had also done some baking and put some Hungarian goulash in the slow cooker for everyone's dinner. That woman was amazing. And Aunt Ruth enjoyed her company as much as her help.

Raven was at his study desk in the dining room in deep contemplation of a dusty old book. I couldn't help but smile, and it melted the edge of my agitation.

'You're back!' I said.

He glared at me and I shrank back, but then he laughed good-naturedly, and warmth spread inside me.

'No harm done, Heather,' he said. 'Every time the curse is triggered, I'm even more determined to find a way to get rid of it.'

I approached with arms wide. 'How about a hug? A platonic one?'

Raven hesitated for a beat before submitting to my invitation. 'I'm glad you're back safely,' I whispered into his ear.

'Thanks.' He lowered his voice as he disengaged from the hug. 'I see Zara is still here.'

'Yeah. I called Abaddon last night and insisted he come himself because she couldn't do the job. He should be here this evening.' *Fingers crossed.* 'Where is Zara, anyway?'

He lowered his head for a moment before replying softly, 'In the back yard... Just sitting there... She didn't respond when I went out to talk to her.' His tone indicated he thought something wasn't right.

From the little I knew of her, that didn't sound like Zara. 'I'll check on her.'

I passed through the kitchen, taking in the wonderful aroma of the slow-cooking stew, and went out the back door into the garden.

The outdoor space was a tranquil retreat, lush and teeming with life from delicate wildflowers to vibrant foliage. The lawn was well kept and lined with mature shrubs and trees to provide shade in the warm summer months. Pools of late afternoon light filtered through the branches, creating a dappled effect. Birds sang in the trees, their sweet melodies making for a peaceful atmosphere.

Though it would be more peaceful if not for the sound of a girl crying in stark contrast to the natural beauty around me.

I hurried across the lawn and found Zara sitting on the other side of a weeping willow.

'What's wrong?' I asked softly as I sat beside her. My knee twinged as I got down to the ground.

She sniffled and wiped her eyes, trying to regain her composure. 'The warlock will be here soon. And he'll be furious with me for wasting the spell scroll.'

'It wasn't your fault.' Well, maybe it was or maybe it wasn't, but it was done now. I managed a reassuring smile.

Zara searched my face for any hint of doubt or disbelief, and she would have seen my concern. 'He won't see it that way,' she whispered, her voice full of fear and trepidation. 'He'll punish me.'

'Don't worry,' I said softly, patting her arm comfortingly. 'I'll talk to him and explain everything. Once he's fixed the mirror and copied the spell book, you can both be on your way home. You'll be back in Berwick upon Tweed by late tomorrow if everything goes well.'

'It won't, though.' Zara's voice trembled.

I remembered that I'd foolishly agreed to pay an extra price for Abaddon to make the journey himself, and I didn't yet know what it would be. My heart sank. How stupid was I? What if Abaddon demanded something outrageous? What if I couldn't pay it?

I couldn't do anything about that now. But Zara's already obvious dread of the warlock's impending arrival only deepened my misgivings.

'Don't you like being Abaddon's assistant?' I ventured.

Zara was silent for a few moments, then said, 'Not really. I mean, it's cool to learn about magic, but he's grumpy the whole time. Even his name means "devil".' Her voice was heavy and tinged with regret.

'How long has he been your mentor?'

Zara shrugged her shoulders and muttered, 'About three years.'

'Three years! How old are you, Zara?'

'Seventeen, I think.'

She's not even sure how old she is. An alarming thought occurred to me. 'What about your family? Do you have any?' I asked cautiously, my mind doing somersaults as I considered the possibilities.

She turned her gaze towards me, her striking grey eyes so intense they made me shiver. There was definitely more to this story than I knew.

Zara seemed to sense my burning curiosity. She raised an eyebrow and said scathingly, 'Why are you asking me so many questions? It's not like I'm your friend or anything.'

A wave of awkwardness washed over me, but I wanted to understand why Zara was so unhappy.

'I'm sorry,' I said, choosing my words carefully. 'I'm worried about you, that's all. It seems you don't like being Abaddon's assistant.'

Zara sighed and looked away. 'I guess so,' she mumbled. 'It's not that I don't enjoy learning magic—I don't like the way he treats me. He's so controlling and demanding. He doesn't care about how I feel, he only wants me to do all his administrative work and keep out of his way, except when he's giving me lessons.' She shook her head sadly. 'I don't understand why he decided to teach me about witchcraft so young.'

What had her family thought of this arrangement? Had they approved or disapproved? Did they even know of it? If she had a family still... and hadn't run away from them.

71

Before I could pose the question, Zara began speaking again. 'The witch's council uplifted me from my mother because they said it was the best thing for my future. I didn't have any say in the matter.' Her voice had taken on a bitter edge, as if she remembered how upsetting it had been at the time. 'My mother could not look after me properly.'

Could not. Past tense. I asked softly, 'Is your mother no longer with us?'

Zara was still for a while, staring deep into the dangling tendrils of the weeping willow we were sitting under. They seemed to move ever so slightly in response to her sorrow. 'She isn't,' she finally replied quietly.

A chill ran through me at the sudden change in the atmosphere. 'I'm sorry to hear that. What about your father? Is he still around?'

Zara laughed bitterly. 'He left my mother many years ago. The warlock is my only family now, and yet he treats me like a servant.'

She started sobbing again. I reached out and put my arm around her shoulders and murmured soothingly, 'He'll be here soon, but I won't let him be mean to you. Don't worry. Everything is going to be all right.'

Zara sniffled, pulling back slightly so our eyes met again.

'That's easy for you to say,' she muttered darkly before wiping away the remaining tears from her cheeks.

Chapter 10

THE WARLOCK ABADDON Masana arrived an hour later, his footfall resounding on the cobblestones with a thunderous boom. When I opened the door, there was no doubt it was him standing on the doorstep.

He cut an impressive figure in his deep purple cloak and hood and towered over me. His eyes were two burning coals that seemed to bore through the shadows of the night. He radiated an air of confidence and power, his gaze commanding and powerful. He had a long, thin nose and sharp angular jaw that made him appear almost menacing. His left hand was curled into a fist, ready for any confrontation, while his right gripped a wooden walking cane topped by a partially hidden elaborate carving.

As Zara had before him, Abaddon swept majestically into the house without waiting for an invitation, his cane rapping on the floorboards. He turned to face me, his cloak dramatically swirling around him like smoke, and gave me a small nod of acknowledgement. 'Heather Nicholls, junior witch, I presume?' he uttered snidely.

I forced myself to remain composed, gritting my teeth against his condescending tone, and smiled awkwardly. 'Why don't you come in?'

'Thank you.' He pirouetted and stormed into the living room. I scurried after him. He blocked Zara's hasty attempt to dash into the kitchen and placed a heavy hand on her shoulder.

'Zara, must I explain everything to you in painstaking detail? You needed only to read that spell scroll once for it to make sense, but you wasted it by using up the spell before you even got here.'

Zara wrenched herself free and weaved past him, too quick for the warlock to catch.

Raven was on his feet immediately and reached the warlock before he could go after her. He put up a restraining arm. 'Leave her be. It was an innocent mistake, something you can easily remedy, I imagine.'

The angry scowl on Abaddon's face softened ever so slightly. 'You are absolutely right, my friend. You must excuse me; it has truly been a lengthy journey, and fatigue has gotten the better of me.'

I smiled reassuringly at him. 'Please take a seat at the table. We are about to serve dinner. Are you hungry?'

Abaddon nodded gratefully. 'I certainly am,' he said, trudging across to the table and taking a seat at one end. He leaned his walking cane against the table leg. The intricate carving on the handle at the top was of a fire-breathing dragon. It complemented its owner's temperament perfectly.

I called Aunt Ruth and Zara. Raven and I went to gather drinks, plates and the meal itself and brought them into the dining room. Aunt Ruth had emerged from wherever she'd been and was introducing herself to Abaddon, who seemed much more relaxed now compared to his initial disposition, perhaps at the promise of imminent food. Zara had cautiously taken the seat farthest away from the warlock without having to meet his gaze when she glanced up.

Dinner started with palpable tension around the table. The warlock directed his stern gaze at me as he broke the silence. 'How long ago did you finish your witch training?' he asked.

'Actually, I'm still working on the assignments,' I said.

'Is that so? Then you're not even a junior witch. You're a trainee.' He raised an eyebrow, and there was no mistaking the sarcasm in his tone.

'Everyone has to start somewhere,' I said, frowning. Did he have to be so patronising?

'I suppose so.' He shrugged.

Aunt Ruth spoke up. 'In our family, witchy abilities do not develop until midlife. I assume it was different for you.'

And Zara, I thought. She remained silent, almost crouched over her meal as if she were trying to make herself invisible in front of Abaddon.

'I mastered the knowledge at an early age. Pardon my observation about your own situation.' The warlock continued to speak with his mouth full.

Raven, who was sitting next to the warlock, said, 'What do you know about lifting curses?'

Abaddon stared at him for a few moments before replying quietly. A shadow passed across his face. 'That is a heavy burden you bear.'

Raven put his cutlery down. 'You can detect it?'

'It surrounds you like a blackened aura. There are but a few chinks of weakness in the outer layer. Lifting it would be... difficult, to say the least.'

'But can it be done?'

Abaddon turned back to his meal, stabbed a baby potato with his fork, and popped it into his mouth. The potato circled in his cheeks as he thoughtfully deliberated over his answer. 'Nothing is impossible,' he finally declared. 'But this...' He paused, as if for dramatic effect. 'This would be close!'

I studied Raven carefully, my gaze lingering on his slumped shoulders, the disappointment thinly veiled behind his visage. Aunt Ruth, sitting next to him, patted his arm reassuringly. 'We will never give up,' she said determinedly.

'I would if I were you.' Abaddon drained his glass. 'Any more wine?'

I reached for the bottle and passed it to him. Dinner was nearing its end, and it was time to get down to business. 'You said something about an additional fee as well as a copy of the spell book as payment for your presence here. What is it you want?'

Abaddon poured himself a full glass of wine and leaned forward eagerly. 'I need *Anacamptis morio*.'

'Never heard of it,' Raven muttered, frowning.

'Is that a person?' I asked. With a name like that, there shouldn't be too many in the phone book.

'It's a plant,' Aunt Ruth said matter-of-factly. 'It's more generally known as the green-winged orchid.'

'That's correct,' Abaddon said.

What would a powerful warlock want with a plant? But it didn't sound too hard, unless it was rare. 'There's a garden centre a short distance away. I can pop in there tomorrow morning before work—'

'That won't do,' Abaddon interrupted in his deep, authoritative voice, which echoed off the walls. 'The plant must be dug from the earth at precisely midnight. Not one minute before or after, or else its magical properties will be rendered useless.'

'The witching hour,' Raven said.

'Okay, then, I'll find some and do exactly that,' I replied resolutely. 'Tonight.'

He shook his head. 'Once the plant is removed, a spell must be cast upon it immediately to preserve the plant and its magic. Otherwise, the magic will die as the plant does.' He eyed me with a haughty expression. 'You are not powerful enough to cast such a spell, but Zara is. She will go with you.'

I glanced sideways at Zara, who nodded slightly, and at Raven, whose gaze flicked briefly to Aunt Ruth. It was clear what he was silently suggesting. He would stay behind so she wouldn't have to stay home alone with the warlock.

'And where do we find this wondrous plant?' I asked curiously.

'They are uncommon, but there are sites within driving distance.'

'I know of one in Kent,' Aunt Ruth said. 'Marden Meadow.'

'Thank you, Aunt Ruth!' I exclaimed. 'Abaddon, does this mean you will fix the magic mirror tonight?'

'Bring me the plant, allow me to copy the spell book, and then I will repair your magic mirror. Not before.' He pushed his chair back. 'Now, if you excuse me, I am quite tired and need to rest. Please show me to my room.'

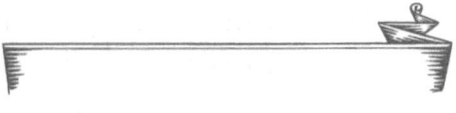

Chapter 11

SHORTLY BEFORE 10 PM, Zara and I turned off Coombe Lane onto the A3. Even at that time of the night, there was plenty of traffic.

'This way?' I asked. Signs to numerous destinations lined the motorway, but they were of little use to me because I didn't know where any of those places were.

'Yes. Keep going. It's miles yet.'

Zara's gaze was glued to her phone, which flickered a faint glow from its screen.

'We have to take the next turnoff,' she finally said, pointing to the illuminated map. 'It joins with the M25.'

I breathed a sigh of relief that we hadn't gone too far and missed the turnoff. With a slight hum, I drove us off the A3 and onto the M25 ring-road motorway, where I clung to the left-hand lane as cars streamed past us like speedy, glittering fireflies.

I glanced over at my passenger. 'Are you used to this many cars? It's not like this where I'm from.'

'I'm pretty much a local here, so yeah, I'm used to it. I grew up in Kingston upon Thames with my mother. I only moved to Berwick upon Tweed much later.'

'To join Abaddon?'

'Yeah.'

'It must feel strange being back here,' I mused aloud.

Zara nodded. 'It's definitely different now.' Looking up from her phone, she turned to me with mild curiosity. 'Where are you from, then?'

'Christchurch in New Zealand,' I replied.

Her eyes widened with surprise. 'Wow, that is a long way away. That's off the coast of Australia, right? Isn't there a bridge between the two countries?'

I chuckled. 'No, no...' I shook my head as I remembered my old home twenty thousand kilometres away—though it may as well have been millions when my daughter and my best friend came to mind. 'There's over two thousand kilometres of ocean between them.'

'Oh, wow,' Zara said, awed. 'It doesn't look that far on the map.'

'Maps can be deceptive. Speaking of maps, are you sure we're still going the right way?'

'Yeah. Keep going. I'll tell you when it's time for the exit.' She peered at her phone. I was thankful she had Google Maps loaded, because she couldn't have read a paper map in the faint light coming through the car windows.

The motorway at night was hypnotic, and I jolted from a semi-glazed state when Zara finally said, 'Take the next one! There!'

I indicated and moved onto the off-ramp. For the next few minutes, Zara navigated us into the country on ever-narrower roads. There was no lighting apart from the car's headlights, and I slowed right down.

'Fuck. We're lost,' Zara said suddenly.

I glanced at her. 'Are you sure?'

'Definitely lost, yes.'

Desperation seized me. 'How can you be so sure we're lost when we can't see a bloody thing and you're using Google Maps to navigate?'

'We should have gone through a village a few miles back. But there wasn't one where I expected it to be.'

'So, where are we, then?' I asked, trying not to panic as the minutes ticked away.

She shook her head and stared at her phone. 'I'll find out.'

I kept driving as we tried to figure out which road we were on and whereabouts on it we were.

Finally, Zara spotted a sign for Marden Meadow. A wave of relief rushed through me as I followed the winding country road until we reached a small car park. Several other cars were parked there, but I couldn't focus on what that might mean—we didn't have time to think about it. It was ten minutes to midnight.

We scrambled out of the car and hurried over to the edge of the meadow. It was a large open space, surrounded by majestic trees and bushes. The stars twinkled brightly in the clear night sky. The moon cast a silvery light over the landscape, giving it a dream-like appearance. A hint of magic tinged the air.

'Quickly,' I urged. 'We don't have much time. We've got to find the orchids.'

A rickety wooden stile crossed a barbed-wire fence. That was our way in.

Zara went first, clambering up and over before letting out an unexpected yelp as her foot landed on the lower step, which wobbled crazily beneath her weight. She swayed back and forth with one leg on either side, hanging on to the post. 'Shit! This isn't safe.' She climbed over cautiously and stepped down to the ground on the other side. 'Be careful.'

I wanted to take my time, but we only had a few minutes left before midnight. I'd never crossed a stile before. It couldn't be as dangerous as Zara said, surely?

Zara nervously hopped from one foot to the other on the far side of the fence as I climbed over, either ready to help support me when I stepped down or to keep out of my way—I didn't know which. The bottom step wobbled dangerously and groaned under my weight, throwing me off balance, and I only prevented myself from falling by gripping the post until I was steady again.

'Be careful!' Zara said, taking a pace backwards as if she expected me to tumble headfirst onto her.

I stepped onto the ground. As soon as my feet touched the grass, a tearing sound filled the air. My top had got caught on the barbed-wire fence, which had ripped a large hole in the fabric near the hemline.

'Fuck! This is one of my favourites.'

'Never mind! Come on! Follow me.' Zara glanced at me with a mixture of amusement and sympathy, then turned and ran into the tall meadow ahead of us.

I followed. Hay grasses swished around my jeans. I couldn't avoid trampling on them as I scanned from side to side in the dim starlight, searching for green-winged orchids before midnight struck.

And, suddenly, there they were, surrounding us—hundreds of blooming orchids, and we'd rushed into the midst of them. I glanced at my phone. Three minutes to twelve.

In the starlight, they were stunning. My heart skipped a beat at the incredible sight. 'They're beautiful!' I exclaimed.

Zara unceremoniously dumped her small backpack atop some of the unfortunate flowers in her haste, crushing their delicate petals beneath its weight, and pulled a trowel and a container from it.

My heart raced as she prepared herself to extract the plants. This part was all up to her. In the background, the sounds of the night seemed to close in: the enchanting hoot of a distant owl, the soothing rustle of grasses blowing in the breeze, the gentle buzzing of insects, some dude quietly chanting in the darkness—

Wait, what?

I cupped one ear in the direction of the murmuring. Yes, someone else was in the meadow, out of sight somewhere in the darkness. I couldn't make out their words, though.

'Zara,' I hissed urgently, my voice barely a whisper. 'We're not alone.'

She didn't even glance up. Instead, she crouched over the patch of orchids, trowel in one hand, container in the other, waiting for the right moment. 'Tell me when it's half a minute to midnight.'

I checked my phone and counted down the seconds until it hit the mark. 'Go!'

She thrust the trowel into the ground with such vigour that I considered asking her if she would do some weeding at home. As she dug ferociously, freeing the roots of several plants, launching dirt into the air with every stroke, her voice cut through the night like an eagle's cry:

A SPELL OF MIRROR MAGIC

Midnight orchids, magic flowers
Rooted deep in ancient powers
I pluck you now with gentle care
And ask that magic linger there

As I lift you from the ground
May your magic still be found
In every leaf, stem and petal
Preserved for the witch's kettle

So mote it be, by my will
You magic orchids, I now thrill
To keep your magic safe and sound
As I remove you from the ground.

Wow. Would I learn spells like that in time? Or would I be limited to weather spells?

As her spellbinding words faded away into the night, Zara hastily swept up the orchids into the container. She closed the lid, jammed it and the trowel into her backpack and threw that on her back with a grin.

I looked up, sensing something. Daunting shadows moved nearby. One of them came to a stop within a few metres of us, sending a chill down my spine. A figure cloaked in a dark, heavy robe, his face hidden by a cowl over his head, a wraith-like figure.

'I've found them! Two witches! Stealing our orchids!' he bellowed with anger.

A man, then, not a wraith.

'Who are they? Farmers?' I asked Zara, though why she would know any better than me, I couldn't imagine.

She let out an exhausted sigh. 'Worse,' she grunted. 'They're druids. We've got to get out of here. Right now.'

The cowled figure loomed closer, and other shadows crowded behind him. 'Stop!' he roared with menacing authority.

Without hesitation, we turned away and ran side by side back the way we had come. I glanced behind. The druids were following, but their long robes encumbered them, so they were not as fast as us.

Thank the stars I'd regained my fitness from all that walking in Richmond Park.

One druid tripped over his robe and fell onto his front in the hay grasses. Another helped him up. I thanked my temperamental luck that I'd chosen to wear jeans and not a long dress.

Zara was several strides ahead of me. She leaped onto the stile, but the rickety step shifted under her weight. She tumbled down the other side with a loud thud.

'Are you okay?' I called, clambering over it more carefully.

'I'm fine,' she replied, already back on her feet. Then her eyes widened in alarm. 'Look out, Heather!'

Out of nowhere, an enormous hand grabbed my upper arm, almost dragging me to a halt. But with a quick jolt of adrenaline, I wrenched myself free and jumped off the stile. 'Run!' I shouted, and we both sprinted toward the car. From behind us came the clomping of boots on the wooden stile.

We reached the car and scrambled inside. I started it and quickly backed out of the park. A wild-eyed cowled face loomed up next to the driver's side window for a moment. I put the car into drive and sped into the night, the figure fading away like a ghost in the darkness.

'We did it!' Zara exclaimed with glee as I grinned at her.

It had been an adventure, all right.

Chapter 12

EARLY THE NEXT MORNING, I dialled Rachel's number. I was tired, but I hadn't spoken to her for a few days, and I wanted to find out how things were going with her new man.

Her face beamed at me from the screen. 'Hey, Heather! How's it going? What've you been up to lately?'

'I'm good. I was out doing a bit of late-night gardening last night.' I chuckled.

'Late at night?' She sounded confused. 'By moonlight? Not dancing naked, were you?'

'LOL. I was decently dressed. It's just that I've been really busy. Anyway, I thought I'd call to find out if you've had another date with Rick since we last spoke, and how it went.'

'Ooh! Have I ever!' Her voice swooned dreamily. 'We went out two nights ago, dinner and dancing. He's such a smooth mover on the dance floor. Especially when he gets going on those Latin numbers... Talk about suave!'

I grinned fondly at my friend's enthusiasm and replied playfully, 'I bet you loved it.' I could almost imagine her twirling around the room as she recounted their recent date.

Rachel chuckled along with me before continuing with an affectionate sigh. 'Yes, he's a smart one, too—plus, who can resist his impressive suits? But...' Her smile faltered. 'There is the fact that he works for a rival firm, which has been giving me minor anxiety attacks lately.'

'That's not promising.'

Rachel sighed. 'Yeah, but I like him, so I'm trying not to think about it.'

'So... there's been nothing to be worried about regarding a conflict of interest?'

She hesitated for a moment before murmuring, 'No... I don't think so.'

'You're not sure?' I pressed.

'Well... Rick stayed the night after our date, and when I got up in the morning, he was already up, dressed and cooking us breakfast.'

'Wow. That was nice of him.' My ex-husband had never done that for me. Not in living memory, anyway.

'Yeah, it was great, but I'd left a pile of confidential case notes on the breakfast bar, and he served up pancakes that were a teeny bit burnt.'

'So, he's not perfect. Unless you think he accidentally let them burn while he was glancing at your case notes?'

'That's what I wondered, yeah.'

'Did you ask him about it?'

'I did, but he said he hadn't noticed them, and he's not good at pancake cooking, so I let it go.'

My eyes narrowed. 'The notes weren't for your super-secret big case, were they?'

'No, only some old client paperwork I'm still working on,' she said.

'That's all good, then. Nothing to worry about.'

'Isn't there?' A note of scepticism crept into Rachel's voice.

'Well, if he said he didn't see them, then he didn't examine them, did he?'

Rachel chewed her upper lip. 'Heather, you forget how cutthroat lawyers can be sometimes. Truth is relative and easily misrepresented.'

I sighed in exasperation. 'You're losing me here, Rach. Are you saying you don't trust him now?'

She hesitated for a moment before responding, her voice full of doubt. 'Oh, I haven't yet determined if I can trust him.'

I frowned. 'Then, maybe it would be better to take this relationship a bit slower rather than diving in like you usually do? Work out if he's trustworthy before you get in too deep?'

'Oh, fuck, no. A catch like him won't wait around while I prevaricate over whether we're right together. It's full steam ahead, or nothing at all.'

'Okay,' I said. 'I only want you to be careful and not get hurt, that's all.'

'I will,' Rachel said. 'Thanks for looking out for me, Heather.'

'No problem. That's what besties are for.'

She laughed. 'Damn right! And besides, I can't break up with him yet. The sex is way too hot to let it go too soon.'

I blushed slightly. 'If you say so.'

'Oh!' She gasped in mock shock. 'You wouldn't believe what he did last time! He—'

'Uh-uh, Rach!' I blurted. 'Remember, my relationship is in the maybe, maybe not, category, after all. Purely platonic.'

'Really?' She exhaled loudly with incredulity. 'Whatever for?'

I sighed. 'It's complicated. I'll explain it to you another time. I have to get ready for work now. Love catching up with you, though!'

'You too.'

We said our goodbyes, and I hung up the phone. Then the ramifications of what I'd said hit me. How I could ever explain to Rachel that every time I kiss the man I fancied, he turns into a raven and flies off?

I YAWNED MY WAY THROUGH our Danish pastry breakfast at Chirtlewood that morning. I hadn't gotten to bed until after 2 am, and I had only had four hours sleep. As I ate, I swigged a mug of strong coffee.

'Late night?' Penny enquired, a wry grin on her face. 'Out on the town with someone special?'

'Unfortunately not,' I said, trying to conceal yet another yawn. No way would I reveal I had spent the middle of the night raiding an old meadow and running from a bunch of irate druids. Sleep had not been easy to come by after that.

'Were you looking into Jane Middlemore's death?' Lydia asked, concern evident in her voice. Was she worried I was trying to leave her out of the investigation?

'No,' I said. 'I was up late doing something for my aunt.'

'You're investigating again? Both of you? I don't know why you bother with that stuff,' Penny said, meaning our amateur sleuthing. 'Didn't the police say it was an accident or a suicide? It's like you're pretending to be private detectives.'

'We'd like to learn more about her. The police may be wrong.' I brushed pastry crumbs from my jacket into my hand and swallowed them.

'Let the woman rest in peace.' Penny's mouth closed in a thin line. She was a private person (and a closet dominatrix, a fact I'd accidentally discovered during my last investigation). She probably thought Lydia and I were poking our noses where they didn't belong.

Lydia ignored Penny's comment. 'I went to the library last night and checked the public records. I found out where Jane lived. Maybe if we pay a visit there, someone could give us more information...'

'Great idea. It's better than simply speculating about what happened.' And the ghosts would want to accompany us, no doubt.

Penny rolled her eyes in mock defeat and crossed her arms over her chest.

Chapter 13

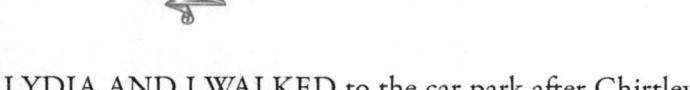

LYDIA AND I WALKED to the car park after Chirtlewood had closed and Penny had left.

'I don't think we can all fit into one car,' I said, evaluating Aunt Ruth's ancient Triumph.

But Lydia's car wasn't much larger. Her eyes widened as she considered the situation. 'The ghosts... they got into the car with you last time?'

'Yes. It seemed the right thing to do.'

She pursed her lips. 'I suppose it is. Though I had the idea they could simply go anywhere they want by simply wishing it.'

'I don't think it works like that,' I explained. 'They can appear and disappear, but not teleport.'

As if on cue, Charlotte and Maisey appeared, barely more substantial than shadows themselves as they passed through Chirtlewood's walls to the outside.

'If the earl's not coming, we'll fit in your car,' I said.

She kept her eyes trained on the manor's spectral inhabitants hovering nearby before finally turning back to me. 'My car?' she asked hesitantly.

'I drove last time, and you know where we're going,' I replied with a smile. 'Besides, you have the nicer car.'

Lydia opened the driver's door and peered inside before glancing at me over her shoulder with genuine fear in her eyes. 'They don't leave ectoplasm on the seats, do they?'

I suppressed a burst of laughter. 'They didn't do that in my car.'

Her doubtful expression faded, and she let out an amused huff. 'Okay.'

Charlotte approached us. 'Yon noble earl hath not come hither,' she explained sadly. 'He appears to be in a rather vexatious disposition this eventide.'

We all got into Lydia's old Toyota, the ghosts climbing into the back seat by passing through the doors. Lydia stared in amazement as they did so.

'Weird, huh?' I said sympathetically before turning towards Charlotte with a mischievous grin.

'My deepest gratitude, Lydia,' Charlotte said. 'Thee hast never deigned to give such a pleasure ere this eventide. Thy knowledge of the finest establishments is commendable.'

Lydia turned in her seat to face the countess. 'Honestly, I didn't even know it was possible for you to leave Chirtlewood. Or that you might want to, for that matter, Charlotte.'

Maisey grinned from the back seat, nodding. 'Oh, aye, prithee. We shalt be of obliging service. I shalt be on me best behaviour.'

Lydia drove us to an address two blocks from the riverfront on the far side of Richmond. I kept an eye on the ghosts to check they weren't fading—as they would if they travelled too far from the place of their death—but they were safe and solid, or at least as solid as ghosts could be.

We exited the car in front of a small dilapidated house that might once have been painted white, but most of the paint had peeled off or faded into grubby grey patches. Cobwebs clung to the corners of the eaves, above which were broken gutters and a moss-patched roof that suggested a picturesque image of abandonment. The windows were coated with a thick layer of dust and dirt.

If the exterior was disheartening, the front garden wasn't any better; weeds were rampant, and a dirt path divided its wildness in two. Loud squeaks accompanied movement in the long grass.

'Someone actually lived here?' I asked, staring at the dismal abode. 'This place must break all the health rules.'

'This is her house,' Lydia said sadly.

Maisey dashed through the fence towards the house. 'Can I wend inside? Prithee?' she called over her shoulder.

'Go ahead. Tell us if there's anything unusual inside,' I said, trying not to envisage what she might find.

'Like in yond other house we entered last time?' Maisey called back.

'What house? What time?' Lydia asked, frowning.

Penny's house. No, this one surely couldn't have those secrets. 'That was after Ronald's murder in the library, but it was a false alarm,' I replied quickly before Maisey could answer.

Fortunately, Lydia dropped the subject. Maisey went inside, passing through the front door as if she were mist. The countess remained with us.

'Let's see if we can find out anything about Jane Middlemore from one of her neighbours,' I suggested.

'But how do you suggest we do it? We're not family or friends of hers, nor are we official police investigators,' Lydia said.

'We'll say we're from Chirtlewood House, and we thought she may have accidentally taken something with her after her visit to the manor.'

'Do you think a neighbour might believe that?'

'We can try.'

Charlotte clapped her hands soundlessly in delight. 'Allow me to observe to what end this shalt come.'

We marched up to the front door of the house on the left, which was much better kept, and knocked.

Before long, shuffling feet approached from within, and the door creaked open. A woman of around seventy answered, drying her hands on a tea-towel. 'Can I help you?'

I started to explain our cover story, but before I could finish, the woman spoke up again. 'Oh, I'm sorry to say Jane passed away a few nights ago. Terrible tragedy it was, too.'

'We read about it,' Lydia said compassionately. 'Were you close?'

The elderly woman shook her head. 'No, no—we were only neighbours. She was a strange woman, I have to say. Kept to herself. Her house is cluttered with curious trinkets and odds-and-ends. But I fed her cat sometimes, if she was away for a day or two. That reminds me, I should do it again this evening.' Sorrow passed over her eyes as she continued. 'Poor little Fluffy. She doesn't understand what happened to her owner.'

'We could come with you while you take care of Fluffy,' Lydia suggested.

'In case the missing item from Chirtlewood is there,' I added quickly. 'We think she may have taken something.'

After a moment of consideration, the neighbour nodded, saying, 'I suppose that will be all right. Wait a moment. I'll get the cat food.'

Two minutes later, she lifted a small plant pot beside Jane's front door and picked up a key, with which she unlocked the house. She showed us inside. While she went to the kitchen to feed the cat and give it some attention, we wandered into the living room.

The walls were faded. Dust bunnies bundled in the corners, and cobwebs dangled in the windows like Halloween decorations. The furniture was dingy and worn, with faded patterned upholstery frayed around the edges. The threadbare carpet was stained with an indeterminate residue. The room itself was a jumbled mess, with piles upon piles of clothes, books and bric-à-brac strewn about. It was as if someone had started sorting through things and given up part way.

I sniffed, trying to put the idea of catching a lingering disease out of my mind. Heavy dust filled my nostrils, along with pungent scents of soiled cat litter seeping from elsewhere in the house. Musty odours of age permeated the room, along with faint traces of incense and herbal tea fragrances. An underlying funk of vanilla candles provided a faint but persistent sweetness.

Lydia's gaze roamed around the room. 'There must be hundreds of trinkets and curios in here,' she whispered, awestruck. 'Maybe even thousands, if every room is like this.'

The countess drifted over to where Maisey stood by an overloaded bookcase. She was pointing excitedly at something hiding in its midst. 'Behold! The pestle is hither!' she exclaimed.

Lydia and I hurried over to take a closer look. As we drew near, Lydia's eyes widened in recognition. 'That thimble and monocle are also from Chirtlewood. They've been missing for months.'

'Jane Middlemore was definitely a kleptomaniac,' I said. 'Well spotted, Maisey.'

The ghost of the young girl grinned, her measles spots spreading wide around her mouth like blots of red ink.

'What insanity hast caused someone to take these meagre things?' the countess asked, levitating to peer more closely at the top shelves. 'They art but paltry baubles.'

'I researched that,' Lydia said. 'People who do that can't resist their impulses to steal items they don't need or want. For them, it's a psychological drive in which the act of stealing is more important than what they actually take, which can be trivial things like this. A pestle without a mortar? Useless.'

'But wherefore didst they commit such an affront?' persisted the countess.

'Apparently, it's because they have feelings of inadequacy or low self-esteem,' explained Lydia, 'or sometimes a need for excitement.'

We all stood there silently for a moment, contemplating the strange urge that drove people to do such things.

'We must take the stolen items back with us,' Lydia said.

'There you are.' Jane's neighbour entered the room, clearly unaware of the ghosts. 'You see, Jane was quite the collector of knick-knacks.'

'We found what we were looking for,' Lydia said, holding up the pestle and other items.

The woman's eyebrows shot up in surprise. 'So quickly? How did you manage that?'

'We're observant,' I said, then changed the subject.

'You must be.' She sighed. 'I don't know what to do with Fluffy now. I suppose she will have to live with me. Especially if Jane's ex-husband doesn't want her.'

'Does her ex live around here?' I asked.

'I don't think so. They split up a long time ago. Their daughter lived with Jane for a while until...' The neighbour sighed heavily again. 'Jane wasn't capable of looking after herself, let alone a child.'

'That must have been hard for her...' I said. A twang of sadness pierced me as I thought of Rose, back at university in New Zealand. 'Jane must have been very lonely.'

'Yes, lonely and depressed. If you're finished here, I should lock up.'

'Yes, we are, thank you,' Lydia said.

The neighbour turned and moved toward the door, but she shivered and rubbed her bare arms as if she'd stepped into an artic breeze. 'It seems cold all of a sudden,' she muttered, looking around warily. 'It must be the thought of the dead.'

No, it's the actual dead. She'd walked right through Charlotte.

Chapter 14

AFTER WE TOOK THE GHOSTS back to Chirtlewood, Lydia and I went our separate ways.

I arrived home at about six thirty in time for dinner. Raven and, surprisingly, Zara had prepared a delicious chicken parmigiana with grilled vegetables.

Dinnertime was a tedious affair. Abaddon's comments about the food did little to lighten the mood: 'This chicken is like chewy dust' and 'I swear this vegetable will choke me if I don't drink soon'. His mocking remarks about everyone else's conversations didn't help either.

No wonder Zara was ill-mannered. She'd picked up the warlock's bad habits.

Afterwards, Aunt Ruth insisted on helping me clear away the dishes. With a wave of her hand, she placed all the plates and glasses into the dishwasher in mere seconds.

'It always amazes me when you do that,' I said.

Aunt Ruth chuckled at my surprise. 'It's only minor magic, dearie,' she said as she wheeled out of the kitchen. 'When I get my magic mirror fixed, I'll show you what real power looks like.'

'Let's get the warlock onto that now,' I said as I made my way towards the living room.

Aunt Ruth rolled in front of me. 'I've put the spell book away in one of the drawers in the cabinet in the living room,' she said. 'I'm afraid if Abaddon gets his hands on the book before he has fixed the mirror, he might take off without doing it.'

'He wouldn't do that, surely,' I protested. 'We have an agreement.'

'Well, I put it out of sight to be on the safe side.' She released my arm and continued to the living room.

The warlock was sprawled in a comfortable armchair, his eyelids drooping as if he might go to sleep any second. I wasn't going to let that happen. I strode closer and leaned over him.

'Abaddon,' I said, my voice loud enough to startle him out of his dozy state.

He jolted awake, eyes wide. 'Wh—what is it?'

'We obtained the green-winged orchids for you last night. Zara, would you kindly fetch the container we brought them back in, please?'

She rose from the floor where she'd been sitting and disappeared down the hall towards her room. I sat on the sofa next to Aunt Ruth, who had transferred across from her wheelchair, and Raven.

Within a few seconds, Zara returned and handed the container to Abaddon without a word. She sat on the floor some distance away.

'Thank you,' he said dryly. 'Did you have any difficulty acquiring them?'

'Only that we got lost along the way, I ripped my top on barbed wire, Zara fell over a stile and we barely escaped from a bunch of maddened druids who were engaged in some kind of weird ceremony.'

Abaddon arched an eyebrow at me as he opened the container to inspect its contents. 'A grove of druids,' he corrected. 'They're not bananas.'

I bit back a retort I might later have regretted.

'Anyway,' the warlock continued, 'avoiding unpleasant complications like those you experienced is precisely why I get other people to perform these tasks for me.'

'I'm not your servant,' I scoffed indignantly.

'Perhaps in this one instance, you were,' Abaddon mused.

My patience with his attitude was as threadbare as Jane's tattered carpets. 'Please perform the spell to fix my aunt's magic mirror,' I said in a strained voice, trying desperately not to tap my foot.

He lifted his head and scrutinised me along his nose. 'Not before I have copied the spell book, as you promised.'

Aunt Ruth shot him a disapproving glare before shaking her finger from side to side in the air. 'No, no, no. We contacted you to perform a service for us. You need to do that first.'

'That's only fair,' Raven added, his voice firm and intense. 'Especially as Heather has already gathered those orchids you wanted.'

It seemed likely that neither of them would back down from their position.

The warlock's expression darkened for a few moments, and then he gave an exasperated sigh. 'Of course. Bring me the mirror.'

'I'll get it,' Raven said, rising before I could say anything. He strode from the room.

He returned shortly after, his biceps bulging beneath his shirt as he carried it effortlessly, despite its size. He stood it on one end, leaning it against the sofa.

Abaddon stared at it in vexation.

'There's only the frame left,' I said needlessly.

'I can see that,' he said dryly. 'Where are the glass fragments?'

'Gone,' I replied sheepishly. Sweat prickled my brow as anxiety swelled within me. 'Is that a problem?'

Abaddon swivelled his head slowly to give me an accusing stare. 'If you had the pieces of magic glass, I could fuse them back into the mirror, and it would be fixed. Without them, I will need a magical gem to transform into the new mirror glass.'

Fuuuuuuck! Now what?

'Hexed and cursed darkness!' Aunt Ruth exclaimed. 'I didn't know that, even though it's my mirror.'

'Damn,' Raven said. 'Does anyone have a magical gem? Just... you know, lying around?'

Silence. Obviously, no one did.

Zara had been quiet since bringing in the container with the orchids, keeping her gaze averted to the floor.

'It is not any old magical gem I require,' the warlock said pompously. 'My craftsmanship must always be of the highest quality, and for that I must have the best components.'

'What do you need us to get?' I asked. 'And where can we find it?' *And how much is it going to cost me?* Dread grew in my stomach.

'You will need to locate a magical moissanite gemstone, the larger the better, which has been imbued with powerful magical properties. It doesn't matter what kind of magic it has, so long as it is full of magic. Then I can enhance and transform the gem into the new glass for the magic mirror.'

'That's a lot of glass from one gem,' Raven said, whistling softly.

'And that,' Abaddon said, emphasising the word 'that' with a pointed finger, 'is why you require a witch or warlock of my inestimable power to do this for you.'

'What's moissanite?' I asked. 'I haven't heard of that before.'

A smirk spread across Abaddon's face. 'Moissanite resembles a diamond in appearance, but it shimmers with far more fire and brilliance because of its artificial composition and structure. It is usually set within a ring.'

'But where can I find a magical one?' I asked. A trace of desperation crept into my voice.

'I know of only one in the entire country,' Abaddon said. 'Fortunately, it is in the possession of a local witch. You might offer to buy it from her.'

'Can you tell us the name of this witch you're talking about?' Aunt Ruth asked.

'Yes,' Abaddon said, scratching his nose absentmindedly. 'Her name is Jane Middlemore.'

Chapter 15

'JANE MIDDLEMORE?' I gasped, reeling in shock.

'Yes. Do you know her?' the warlock asked, leaning in closer.

'I've met her once.' My mind was a swirling kaleidoscope of confused thoughts. Did Abaddon know her himself? Should I tell him she was dead, that the police were investigating and they did not know if it had been an accidental death or something more deliberate?

'Are you okay, Heather?' Raven asked, taking my hand in both of his. His concerned gaze met mine, full of compassion. 'You've gone pale.'

Aunt Ruth watched me intently, her brows knitted together with concern.

Zara stood up. 'I'll get you a glass of water.' She hurried from the room.

I forced a smile onto my face. 'I'm fine,' I lied. It was the world's most common lie. I didn't want to explain the whirlpool of jumbled thoughts and emotions going through my mind.

'Are you positive?' Raven pressed me. I'm sure he sensed I was battling something distressing.

'Yes.' I took a deep breath and pushed away the chaotic thoughts. Focus. What's the most important thing here? Aunt Ruth's health, obviously. She may have a chance to heal herself using a spell from the spell book once Abaddon has fixed her magic mirror. But the warlock could do that only by transforming the gem.

Therefore, what mattered now was obtaining the particular moissanite gem he'd spoken of. That was paramount. Saying Jane Middlemore was dead would only complicate matters. I could always tell him later.

'How much is the precious gem worth?' Aunt Ruth asked. 'Would the witch be willing to sell it to us?'

'I have no idea,' Abaddon said. 'If not, you could always search for another one. In Ireland, maybe. Or France. I believe a few exist in those countries.'

'We could use the Witchnet,' I said absentmindedly, my thoughts still on Jane Middlemore.

'The quickest thing would be to approach this Jane Middlemore,' Raven said. 'She's local, so we could ask her tomorrow. Then we'd know whether she's willing to sell and at what price. If she is, that will save us from traipsing across half of Europe looking for one.'

An idea percolated in my brain and I said, 'Leave it with me. I'll handle it.'

'Do so quickly,' Abaddon said. 'I want to return home as soon as possible.'

He had no argument from me about that.

I WAITED UNTIL TEN o'clock that evening to put my plan into action. Everyone else had headed off to bed for the night. In my room, I changed into black clothes with black sneakers and grabbed a flashlight, trying not to dwell on what I was getting myself into.

When I emerged from my room, I was startled. Raven was leaning against the wooden banister on the landing, waiting.

'Going somewhere?' he asked me, smiling.

'Out for a walk. Late-night strolls help clear my mind,' I replied breezily. Would he believe me?

He raised an eyebrow. 'At this time of the night with that outfit? You'll be invisible. You're dressed like an extra on some spy movie set. What are you really going to do, Heather?'

I couldn't stop the small twitch of my lips as I realised how obvious my intentions must have been. 'I'm sure you can guess.'

'Want me to come with you?' he asked, his smile widening.

'Thanks, but I'll go on my own. I've got this.'

Raven gave me an understanding nod and wished me luck. 'Stay safe. Call if you need help.'

'I will. Thanks, Raven.'

I went downstairs and got into the car without delay in case he changed his mind and insisted on coming with me. I didn't like what I was about to do, but there was no alternative if I wanted to fix that bloody mirror as quickly as possible.

I couldn't offer to buy the magical moissanite gem from Jane Middlemore because she was dead. And it might be months before her relatives—if they could be found—dealt with her estate. I couldn't afford to wait for that. I needed it now.

The warlock wouldn't wait months, merely days at the most. And Aunt Ruth didn't have months either. Her cryptic message about September the third being her last day rang in my ears like a death knell. I'd never been able to get any details about that from her.

My brain hurt from the stress of everything. *One thing at a time, Heather.*

I had to think fast. I hadn't come this far just to give up now. If only there was a way to uncover the gemstone without having to sift through thousands of worthless trinkets and bric-à-brac at Jane's house. That would be like looking for a blade of straw in a Victorian clothing sweatshop. I could spend all night there and not find it.

I drove towards Richmond at first, but deviated after an idea struck me. A few minutes later, I pulled up outside Chirtlewood and got out of the car. The chilly air embraced me with its icy tendrils. Clouds obscured the moon and stars. In the darkness, the manor house loomed like a giant shadow before me, menacing rather than inviting, as it appeared in the daylight.

Was I wasting my time here? I wanted to ask Charlotte and Maisey for their help, but there was no guarantee I would find them or that they would respond if I called. Did ghosts sleep? And if they slept, did they have dreams? Or nightmares? And of what? How would they react if I disturbed them at night?

My head was abuzz with questions, but I couldn't find any answers.

A barking dog interrupted my thoughts. My heart skipped a beat. Was that a security patrol?

It wasn't. A familiar border collie came bounding towards me, yapping happily.

I reached down to pat him, but my hand went straight through him. 'Hi, Scruffles,' I said with a smile. 'I wish I could give you a cuddle. I need some help. Is anyone up and about?' *I really should find out if they sleep.*

The ghost dog gave a few excited barks before bolting off. He leaped straight through the outer wall of Chirtlewood House, disappearing inside.

I waited for several minutes and let out a little shiver as the night chill set in around me.

Eventually, Maisey stepped through the wall and approached, followed closely by Charlotte. I shivered at the sight of Maisey in her tatty, thin dress or nightgown. The fabric was so frayed I couldn't identify what it used to be. But at least she didn't seem cold.

Charlotte was dressed as usual in her open high-necked chemise with green sleeves. 'Heather,' she said. 'What endues thee hither this night?'

'I thought it might be fun if I could get your help searching for something, if you would like another outing.'

'Oh, aye, prithee,' Maisey said, a mischievous glint in her eye.

'Ooh!' Charlotte exclaimed at the prospect of a late-night escapade. 'Oh, aye! How terribly lovely! Pray tell, what is it thee seek?'

'A gem, possibly concealed in that house we visited earlier this evening. But this time, we will have to sneak inside. Or I will, I mean.'

'What grand jewel hath enamoured thee so?'

'Let's go, and I'll tell you.'

Maisey had already entered the car through the back window. Charlotte passed through the passenger door while I got into the car. I drove off towards Richmond.

'It's a moissanite gem,' I said. 'Possibly on a ring.'

'I never hast heard of such a thing ere,' Charlotte said, 'and I hadst the distinct pleasure of owning a considerable and diverse trove of jewels in my mortal life.'

I glanced behind at Maisey. She may never even have seen a gemstone during her gruelling peasant life. How did she feel about the huge social gap between her and the countess? In life, they wouldn't ever have crossed paths socially. Yet after death, all that matters is friendship.

'It's like a diamond,' I explained, 'but larger and with more flashing colour and brilliance.'

'My word, 'tis truly a marvel! How hast mine eyes never behold such a sight?' Charlotte asked.

'It is an artificial gemstone, produced by artisans.'

'Magic,' Maisey whispered.

I chuckled. 'Jewels like that are made with technology, but the particular gemstone we need to find has magical properties too.'

I parked outside Jane's house and checked the house where we'd spoken to her neighbour. The lights were off. The woman must have gone to bed.

'Let's go,' I whispered, closing the car door as quietly as a soft breeze through a tree in winter.

I shone the flashlight onto the ground as we crept towards the house. Sure enough, the front door key was still hidden beneath the plant pot. The ghosts had already entered through the wall. I envied their ability to pass through solid objects and let myself in with the key.

'Let's each take a room and search carefully, but quickly, so we're out of here as soon as possible,' I said. 'Remember, it may be hidden. The lady who lived here collected a lot of trinkets, but this gemstone was valuable.' A pang of guilt hit me like a needle of ice. I was engaging in burglary. Not exactly the good behaviour I was brought up to follow.

Charlotte headed for the bedroom, and Maisey ventured into the kitchen. I remained in the living room, my gaze sweeping around the cluttered shelves and glass-fronted cabinets. This could take a while.

With a deep breath and my trusty flashlight in hand, I started with the bookcases, examining each shelf carefully, lifting or moving aside larger pieces to see what lay behind them. Usually, that was more stuff. I found everything from tiny plastic figures, foreign coins, corks from wine bottles, parts of a clock, scraps of fabric, cutlery, used-up makeup, hairpins and a variety of things I couldn't even guess the purpose of. It was like a treasure chest with junk instead of actual treasure.

After twenty minutes had passed, a gasp of surprise came from the kitchen, and I rushed in, with Charlotte floating along in my wake.

'What is it?' Charlotte asked eagerly.

'I bethink I hast found it!' Maisey exclaimed, pointing to a shelf behind a row of mugs. Sure enough, a small wooden box, with the top slightly displaced, lay nestled between two earthenware vessels.

Maisey couldn't open it, being of spectral form, but she had peeked inside through the small gap.

'There's a gemstone inside!' she said.

We crowded around eagerly as I carefully opened the box and pulled out the most beautiful gem I had ever seen! It was round and sparkly with flashes of blues, greens, and pinks that danced with life when the light from my flashlight hit them. Its beauty was mesmerising—much more intense than any diamond. 'This is it! This must be the moissanite gem!'

We stood motionless, staring in awe at the brilliant object, until Charlotte finally spoke. 'My goodness... 'tis exquisite.'

Maisey's voice quivered in awe as she whispered, 'Aye, 'tis so pretty.'

'Well done,' I said, slipping the precious gemstone into my pocket. 'Now, we had better go.'

Guilt gnawed at me once more as I moved into the hall. Once I went through the front door, I would be a thief. There was no changing that.

My heart raced faster, thumping like a half-crazed heavy metal drummer.

I reminded myself I didn't have a choice. We exited the house. I locked it and put the key back where I'd found it. The street was clear. A few lights were on in houses further down the road, but none nearby, and no one seemed to notice us as we made our escape.

A minute later, I drove back towards Chirtlewood House with Charlotte and Maisey. 'Thank you both,' I said. 'I couldn't have done this without you.'

''Twast my pleasure,' Charlotte replied.

'That was fun. Can we wend out thieving again?' Maisey said.

'No,' I said firmly. 'This was a one-time thing only. And I'll pay for the item somehow.'

I dropped my ghostly companions off at Chirtlewood and waved goodbye. It was almost eleven o'clock. The whole mission had taken less than an hour.

Tomorrow, I'd get the moissanite ring valued by a jeweller. Maybe I could go after work or slip out to Richmond at lunchtime. Once I knew what it was worth, I'd save up the money and pay it to Jane's heirs anonymously. It wouldn't completely assuage my twinges of guilt, but it would help.

With a plan in place and a flicker of hope burning in my heart, I drove off into the night, heading home.

Tomorrow, the warlock will have no excuse not to fix that damned magic mirror.

Chapter 16

I ENTERED THE HOUSE quietly so as not to wake anyone up. A glimmer of light spilled out from the living room, and I froze mid-step. Someone was still up. Raven, maybe?

A low muttering came from the living room. I couldn't make out the words, but it wasn't Raven's voice.

I crept closer and peeked around the doorframe. Abaddon was hunched over something on the antique mahogany cabinet. Something about his behaviour made me suspicious. I squinted in the darkness, taking in his sea-blue flannel pyjamas adorned with cartoon rockets—definitely not his usual attire. And he was peering intently at an enormous book lying open before him.

The witch's spell book! He must have searched for it after he'd thought everyone else had gone to bed. Luckily, though I'd gone out, I'd returned at the right time to catch him.

Something within me screamed to rush in, challenge him and demand he tell me what he was up to, but he might bluff an answer. It would be wiser to watch what he did. I edged away from the open door and melted into the shadows of the hallway. From my hiding place, I once more peeked around the doorframe at Abaddon from the shadows, like a patient spy in a movie.

A SPELL OF MIRROR MAGIC

Abaddon pulled a large leather-bound book from the inside of his pyjamas and laid it quietly next to the spell book.

I raised an eyebrow, eyes glued to the warlock. What was he doing? Was he sneakily about to copy the spell book without asking? I held my breath and remained motionless, not wanting to make a noise that might give my presence away.

The warlock grabbed the daisies from a small vase on the cabinet and placed them on the table with a satisfied smirk. He gave the now-empty vase a pointed glare, his fingertips gradually glowing blue as energy swirled around them. To my amazement, the delicate vase cracked and split into two pieces, each transforming into a unique object before my eyes.

My fingers on the doorframe turned white as I clung to it even more tightly, captivated.

The smaller piece became a large feathered quill, floating and twirling by an unseen force. The remainder of the vase morphed into a transparent inkpot filled to the brim with black ink glistening like liquid ebony.

Abaddon raised his hands in triumph, exuding haughty confidence. He intoned a spell:

With quill and ink, I draw these lines
To copy spells and lore divine
From ancient tome and hallowed page
I call upon the copy mage

With speed and care, let these words flow
Into this book, let them form and grow

As I have read, so it shall be
A faithful copy, bound to me

By the power of earth, air, fire and sea
This spell book be copied, so mote it be!

The quill danced in the air, dipping itself into the ink pot with a flourish, before it flew to the volume Abaddon had placed next to the witch's spell book. It scrawled at lightning speed as if held by an invisible hand that wrote at an impossible pace, frequently dipping itself back into the inky depths for more.

My mouth hung agape, and I suppressed a gasp. The quill bounced a little in the air, as if pausing for breath, when the page turned, and, in perfect synchronisation, a page of the spell book turned as well.

The process continued apace with pages filled with words and symbols in mere seconds by the racing quill, then flipping over to begin anew on a fresh side.

Ten minutes later, both books shut themselves with a soft thud, and Abaddon grinned widely.

I had remained hidden, but now it was time for me to announce my presence. I stepped into the room and switched on the lights, illuminating the clandestine scene before me. Abaddon jumped, clearly startled, and his face flushed red.

'I saw what you were doing,' I said accusingly, narrowing my eyes.

There was no point in the warlock denying it. He was caught ink-handed, even though he hadn't written a single word himself.

'It's not what you think,' Abaddon stammered, squirming under my accusatory glare.

'It appeared you were copying the spell book, which Aunt Ruth had put away out of sight. If it wasn't that, then what was it you were doing?' I demanded, hands firmly planted on my hips. I wouldn't let him talk his way out of this.

He exhaled loudly and shifted his weight from one foot to the other. 'All right. That's what I was doing. But I merely wanted to save time. I swear I'll fix your aunt's mirror tomorrow, if you give me the gem I asked for. Then Zara and I won't need to keep you any longer since I already have my own copy of the spell book.'

'I have the gem with me now, but copying the spell book only took you a few minutes—hardly a delay if you'd waited until tomorrow. Plus, since we were keeping the book hidden until you completed the task, you must have snooped around for it. Do you make a habit of going through old ladies' drawers?'

His lips curled into a sneer. 'How do I know you would have allowed me to copy the spell book after I fixed your blasted mirror?' he hissed irritably. 'How could I even be sure the spell book existed in the first place?'

I crossed my arms over my chest and levelled him with a steely gaze. 'I promised you. I made a bargain with you.'

Abaddon stiffened and his nose scrunched up in the air. 'Bargains and promises are easily made and as easily broken,' he muttered darkly.

'I don't break my promises!' I retorted indignantly.

He gave a derisive snort. 'How would I know that? I've only just met you.'

I took a deep breath to control my simmering anger and give myself time to gather my thoughts. 'We're not getting anywhere with this. I understand you're mistrusting. How about this: you keep the copy you made of the spell book a few minutes ago, but you must promise to fix the magic mirror as soon as possible tomorrow. And you must make another copy of the book immediately for us.'

Abaddon nodded in agreement. 'I can do that.'

He reached inside his pyjamas and pulled out another large, leather-bound volume with a flourish, as if producing it from thin air.

'How's it possible for you to have such huge books tucked into your pyjamas?' I asked incredulously. 'I didn't see any lumpy bits.'

The warlock chuckled deeply—a rumbling sound like thunder pealing off a distant horizon. 'Is that so?' His dark eyes twinkled with amusement. 'It's a simple transmogrification trick. When I put the books in there, they shrink. When I take them out, they revert to their original size.'

I watched, transfixed with wonder, as Abaddon methodically repeated the copying process I'd witnessed before. Observing from such a close distance was exhilarating. The sound of the quill scratching against the heavy paper made me shiver in excitement. Every stroke of ink dried instantly, as if frozen in place.

After ten minutes, Abaddon placed the completed copy in my arms. It was heavier than I expected. Perhaps magic had an atomic number and therefore possessed weight.

He put the original spell book back in the drawer in the cabinet and nodded goodnight to me.

'I will see you tomorrow to fix the mirror,' I said, still mesmerised.

He smiled pleasantly and took his own copy with him as he headed for the hall.

I sat for a while, leafing through the book. Most of it was unintelligible to me. The symbols were fascinating, though I couldn't figure out what they stood for. Maybe Aunt Ruth could explain. Maybe she might decipher this archaic text and even teach me some true witchy ways in time. If only she had time.

Gently cradling the book under my arm, I headed to the kitchen to make myself a cup of white hot chocolate.

I FINISHED MY LATE-night drink and settled into bed with a book. My phone trilled with an incoming video call, startling me. I glanced at the time. It was past midnight. Had Rose mixed up the time zone difference again?

It wasn't Rose. It was Rachel, calling from her work phone. I snatched it up and answered.

'Hi, Rachel. Is everything okay? It's late here, and we spoke only this morning. Is something wrong?'

'Hi, Heather. Everything's fine.' Rachel's face beamed at me from the screen. She was in her lawyer's office, in a flash new building constructed following the earthquakes in Christchurch a few years ago. 'Sorry for calling so late, but I saw you were online, and I have some super exciting news for you—your house sale settled this morning.'

Pure relief coursed through me—that was a massive weight off my mind. 'Oh, Rachel, thank you so much for seeing that through. That's fantastic news!'

Rachel continued. 'No problem. I've wired your share of the proceeds to your UK bank account, as you requested. You should receive that in the next couple of days.' She paused. 'Have you heard from Terry lately?'

'Not directly,' I replied. 'Rose told me he's moving to Wellington to start up his own business using his share of the house sale proceeds. Can you believe it? And he wants to crash at her flat until he sorts his shit out.'

'I don't envy her. She's sharing with other students, isn't she?'

'Yes. There's literally no room for him, but I'm sure you remember how entitled he is.' I couldn't forget it.

'I do.' Rachel smiled, her eyes glinting knowingly. 'So, back to the legal matters. That was the last of the shared assets with Terry. Now it's a matter of waiting until the two years are up and you can apply for your divorce.'

I grinned. 'Now Terry's got no reason to be in my life unless it's something to do with Rose. I should have got out of the marriage years ago. It took me too long to realise that he'd stopped caring and was taking me for granted.'

'Perhaps,' Rachel agreed, her expression sympathetic, 'but at least you've gone through with it now.'

'And now I can move on with my life and my new career,' I said firmly.

She nodded. 'That's the attitude, girlfriend!'

'Looking forward, thinking positively, right? Not backwards at the pit of my marriage, at how pointless and empty most of those years were.'

'That's right.' Rachel paused, her gaze narrowing as she studied my face. 'Is everything okay, Heather? You're... not your usual self. Is it stress about the house sale? That's over now. It's not some trouble with Rose, is it?'

'I'm tired, that's all,' I muttered defensively, avoiding eye contact.

'Well, I'm not surprised, given your late-night activities.'

'What?' Panic stabbed through me. What was she referring to? How could she know about me stealing the moissanite gemstone only two hours ago from halfway around the world?

'Your midnight gardening,' Rachel clarified. 'That's why you're tired, isn't it?'

'Oh, that.' I exhaled sharply. 'Maybe. And I'm worried about Aunt Ruth. She still hasn't regained any movement in her legs. She might never do.'

'That's awful. I'm sorry to hear that. You're doing everything you can for her, I know. Remember to look after yourself, too.'

I nodded sadly. 'I'm investigating another death,' I blurted out.

Rachael's eyes widened in surprise. 'What? Another murder? Are you trying to become a detective in your spare time?'

I chuckled weakly and ran a hand through my hair. 'Oh, we don't yet know if it's a murder. It might have been an accident or...' My voice trailed off.

'And who are "we"? Don't tell me you've joined a local vigilante gang?'

I tried to laugh, but my chuckle turned into a sob, which I covered up as best as I could. *Calm down. Deep breaths.* I'd let the pressure get to me.

'Heather? Are you sure you're okay?'

I shook my head before I could stop myself. 'Only tired. That's all. I'd best go to sleep, Rach. Thanks so much for calling me about the house. It's such great news.'

Rachael pursed her lips determinedly and peered at me through the screen. Her lawyer's emotional intelligence would have gone into overdrive, trying to figure out what was up with me.

'I'm going to call you back in two or three days and see how you are. I'm worried about you, girlfriend. You're not yourself. I can see something is troubling you, and I want to get to the bottom of it and help you if I can. Remember—whatever it is, you don't have to go through it alone.'

'I know. Thanks, Rach. Let's talk again soon.'

We ended the call.

How could I possibly explain to Rachel—the logical, professional lawyer—that my life had taken an unexpected supernatural turn and now included learning witchcraft, stealing things for warlocks and taking ghosts on excursions?

Rachel had been my best friend for many, many years. Back to our school days. Though our lives went down different paths—hers being a high-flying job and no family commitments, and mine being the complete opposite—we stayed close because we'd always been completely open and honest with each other.

Now I was betraying that trust by not sharing with her the paranormal elements of my new life. I was lying by omission by pretending otherwise. How long could I keep doing that?

I couldn't tell Rachel what was really going on for me... She would think I was crazy.

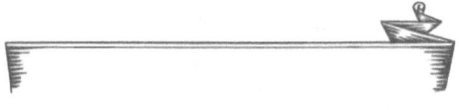

Chapter 17

MY ALARM RANG AN HOUR early, and I rose immediately, despite my grogginess from lack of sleep. I dressed and went downstairs for a cup of coffee. It seemed that no one else in the house was awake yet.

After putting the original spell book in the car, I drove to Richmond. A fox ran along the footpath, probably startled by my car while it was rummaging for food. Thousands of foxes lived in greater London. Foxes were rumoured to be cunning. I needed some of that myself.

I wanted to have another look at the location where Jane Middlemore's body had been found floating in the river. That was probably not where she'd entered the river, though. Had the police located that spot? Could I?

After parking nearby, I strolled towards the area where Jane's body had been fished out of the river. It was no longer cordoned off, if it had ever been. It was as if nothing had happened there. There weren't even any flowers or notes left by well-wishers to mark her sudden departure from life. A pang of sadness hit me for Jane, whom I hadn't known. Was there no one to remember her?

With hope that something—anything—would catch my eye, I walked upstream along the Thames path, scrutinising the walkway and the ground between it and the river.

What exactly should I search for? Might there be something marking where Jane waded in? Footprints or slip marks on the riverbank? Maybe a note pinned to a tree that still lay undiscovered?

Yeah, unlikely.

If I walked slowly for forty minutes, scouting carefully, I could stride back in twenty and get to work on time. At my age, walking for exercise was my friend—especially with all the pastry breakfasts I had.

But where and how had Jane entered the river? I almost called Lydia to see if she would join me on my quest for clues, but it was far too late. Soon, I'd have to turn back if I was to get to work on time.

I continued on, the wind rippling past me like a faint whisper. A few other people were out walking, some power-walking with faces full of grim determination, some strolling arm-in-arm and others exercising their dogs. Light penetrated the leafy trees in places, creating dancing sunspots on the path. The river sparkled like diamonds—or perhaps moissanite—in the early morning sunlight.

After thirty minutes, I arrived at a part of the river where the bank was slightly higher and steeper. Broad trees cast deep shadows across the path and the edge of the river, and the temperature dropped a few degrees. I halted in my tracks. Something about this particular spot chilled me, and it wasn't just the shade.

I examined the riverbank for clues. The grass on the high bank had worn away, and dried mud remained in its place. I stepped over and checked the shoreline carefully—it appeared as though something had disturbed the ground there. The mud appeared scuffed, and—there! A footprint. Or a boot print, to be exact. With something underneath, barely visible between two mud ridges.

What, was I a forensic scientist now? Was I imagining what I'd wanted to find? Yet the marks in the mud did look like the heel of a boot.

Out of nowhere came a rustling sound, and a smartly dressed figure emerged from behind a billowing willow tree near me. Upon seeing the silhouette, I gasped in fright until recognition dawned.

'Inspector Pentecost!' I exclaimed breathlessly.

'Ms Nicholls.' She chuckled. 'What a pleasant surprise to find you here. Do you come here often?'

I arched an eyebrow. 'Are you hitting on me?'

She laughed. 'Not at all. I merely thought it was quite a coincidence that I find you here a few days after someone went into the river at this particular spot and died.' She squinted her eyes at me as if trying to read my mind. 'So, why are you here?'

'You know me,' I said with a shrug. 'I'm super curious—which is often mistaken for nosiness—and I also like walking. It seemed natural to combine the two.'

'And that brought you to this precise location, I see.'

I wasn't going to try to explain that. 'So, this is the spot where Jane Middlemore went into the river?'

'Yes, it is,' the inspector replied crisply. 'I wanted to have another look at it.'

'How do you know this is the right place?'

Inspector Pentecost pointed at the riverbank. 'A police search found one of her shoes halfway down there.'

That confirmed my suspicions. I'd found the spot where Jane had gone over. Maybe it was witchy intuition or something.

The inspector continued. 'You paused for an awfully long time right here too, Ms Nicholls. Care to explain what made you investigate this particular area? Out of all the places around here that might have caught your interest?'

Her tone wasn't accusatory. Perhaps she was fishing for an explanation for what appeared to be an unlikely coincidence.

'It's pretty along the river around here,' I said guardedly.

'Come on, Ms Nicholls. Or shall I call you Heather? We're bumping into each other often enough to warrant sending each other cards at Christmas. If people still do that sort of thing.'

'Heather is fine.' Is she going to keep pressing me? 'You know I fancy myself as a private investigator...'

Inspector Pentecost let out a chuckle. 'I remember that about you well enough. What makes you think there is something to investigate here?'

I sighed. 'It's just a feeling I have, Inspector. And... I'm not sure, but I think that's the remains of a boot print there in the dried mud.' I gestured toward it.

Inspector Pentecost nodded. 'You're right. We got a cast of it. It wasn't from Jane Middlemore's footwear, though. However, it doesn't confirm that anyone else was with her when she died. Maybe someone unconnected stopped by at a completely different time, admiring the river view. Nor do we know how she ended up in the river. She may have fallen in or jumped in deliberately.'

'Maybe there actually was a second person involved, and that's their boot print,' I suggested tentatively, trying to shake off a creepy sensation that crawled like spiders along my spine.

'It's possible, but as I said, we can't be sure of it,' the inspector said thoughtfully. 'We haven't discounted foul play yet.' Her gaze swept the trees and shrubs lining the riverbank before continuing. 'But your intuition is right, Heather—something doesn't add up here. People don't go for a swim in the Thames at night under normal circumstances, especially alone. You would have to be crazy to swim in the Thames at any time, in my opinion.'

'Maybe someone saw something,' I suggested. 'A local person may have noticed Jane out walking that night. They could say whether she was alone or with someone else.'

Inspector Pentecost nodded. 'My thoughts exactly. I've had constables out asking locals if they saw her. It's a slow process. Often, no one is home when our officers knock on their door. It'll take time to cover the whole area.'

I crouched to inspect the boot print again. Yes, there was definitely something underneath it. Only a tiny white patch was visible. I looked up. 'Inspector, this might simply be a piece of rubbish, but—'

In two quick strides, she was by my side, bending over to see what I was referring to. 'You're right. It must have been uncovered when the mud dried.' She fished in a pocket and brought out a pair of tweezers. Carefully, she extracted the item and showed it to me. It was a bottom corner torn from a photograph. Part of a woman's dress was visible.

'That's no use,' I said. 'It's too small. You can't even see who it is.'

'You never know,' the inspector said. 'Any little thing might be important.' She took a small zip-lock bag from a pocket and dropped the partial photograph inside.

I watched with interest, then said, 'I have to go, Inspector. I'm due at Chirtlewood soon.'

She smiled. 'I appreciate your thoughts, Heather. You're a smart woman.'

I couldn't help but blush from such kind words, so different from our first encounters. 'Thank you. Maybe we should talk again soon?'

'I'm sure we will. Have a good day.'

'You too.'

I turned and strode back the way I'd come, afraid I might be late for work, or, rather, the pastry breakfast prior to opening the house for visitors.

Maybe Lydia and I could talk to a few people around here later and see if we could uncover a few unknown facts. It's great that Inspector Pentecost cares about what happened to Jane too, but Lydia and I were witches. And we had ghosts as friends. That gave us an advantage in the investigation.

Chapter 18

AT CHIRTLEWOOD, I TOLD Lydia that I'd brought the borrowed spell book with me. As I slid it back into its shelf space in the library, a sad memory of Ronald, our visiting retired researcher, entered my mind. He'd hunted for this particular book for ages. I remembered his joy at finding it and our horror at what had followed.

I put those gloomy events out of my mind and set to work, watching over visitors to the manor house and answering their questions if they had any. This was so much better than my old teaching job in New Zealand. Visitors here actually wanted to learn history.

Once the manor was closed for the day, Lydia, I, Charlotte and Maisey piled into Lydia's car with the enthusiasm of school children embarking on a class field trip.

Lydia and I planned to ask locals if they'd seen Jane Middlemore on the evening of her death. Clearly, our ghost companions couldn't be any help with the questioning, but once they knew we were continuing with our investigation, some of them insisted on coming along anyway, even if only to watch. And Maisey was extremely observant and might spot something Lydia and I missed. The earl elected to stay home with Scruffles instead.

In the car, I told them about how I encountered Inspector Pentecost by the spot where Jane had entered the river.

'How did you know that was the right spot?' Lydia asked.

'I sensed it somehow, and I found a footprint.'

'But that could have been anyone's footprint.'

'Yes,' I said, as we reached the outskirts of Richmond village, 'but I noticed something in the mud. Before I could pick it up, the Inspector came up to me. She pulled it out. It was the torn corner of a photograph, and she placed it in an evidence bag.'

'Could you see anyone in the photo?'

'No... unfortunately not.'

Lydia fell silent as she processed this for a few moments.

I pulled up along a row of houses built in the 1930s on the opposite side of the river from where Jane had gone into the water. We started knocking on doors and soon found ourselves talking to a friendly elderly man named Mr O'Grady.

'I was in my bedroom at night when I noticed two figures strolling along the riverbank,' he began, his voice quivering with emotion. 'It was too dark for me to make out any details, but I could tell they were walking very close together.'

'Like they knew each other, maybe?' Lydia asked.

I slow-blinked. *Leading question.*

'Yes. Then they detoured off the path and went behind that willow tree there.' Mr O'Grady pointed in the direction of the tree where I'd spoken to the inspector.

'And what happened next?' I prompted.

Mr O'Grady paused, his eyes widening as if seeing it all over again in his mind's eye, and swallowed before continuing. 'Only one of them came out from behind that tree. I watched for a while because I was curious, but I never saw the other person. I remember I felt a chill run down my spine. And then I dismissed it. It was dark and my old eyes sometimes play tricks on me.'

'What time was that, Mr O'Grady?' Lydia asked.

'It was about nine o'clock, as I recall. I was heading off to bed, and I wanted to see the moonlight on the river.'

'I shalt wend inside,' Maisey whispered, though of course Mr O'Grady couldn't hear her, anyway. She dashed in and ran upstairs.

As we thanked Mr O'Grady and said our goodbyes, I remembered Maisey was still inside the house. What was she up to?

After a minute or so, Maisey emerged from the house like an adventurer emerging from a tomb, passing directly through the now-closed front door. She caught sight of us waiting on the footpath and raced over. 'I made sure his tale wast true. His chamber window grants a grand behold of the willow yonder.'

'Thanks, Maisey,' I said. 'I appreciate you checking that.'

We continued going house to house and spoke to a few more locals who had seen Jane that evening, but none of them could provide any new information.

We eventually decided to call it a day and headed back to Chirtlewood, slightly deflated, yet determined to keep investigating somehow.

'Thankee for another exciting journey,' Maisey said, beaming.

Charlotte hung around, deep in thought. 'Allow us endeavour to locate yond individual if it be possible.'

'Oh, that could prove difficult.' Lydia groaned and rubbed her temples. 'We don't have any sort of description. It could be anyone.'

'Yeah, I know,' I said. 'One thing we should do, though, is tell the inspector what we found out.'

'Are you sure?'

'Yes. It's important, and she might give us information in return.'

Charlotte seemed perplexed. 'I doth not understand how we can find this other person. We couldst ask everyone in the village, but it might not be any of those folk.'

'And there's no way of knowing if someone is lying,' Lydia said.

'I'll text Inspector Pentecost and tell her about Mr O'Grady and what he saw,' I said. 'Let's see if that gets us anywhere. Or gets her anywhere, at least.'

Lydia stretched and stifled a yawn. 'Let us know what happens. I'm exhausted after all that sleuthing. See you tomorrow, Heather. And you, too, Charlotte, if you're around.'

'I'm at each moment hither,' the countess replied with a wry smirk. 'Thy every move in this house is beknown to me.'

'Comforting,' I said with a hint of sarcasm. There was no privacy from these ghosts.

I ARRIVED HOME AROUND eight o'clock that evening, and the house seemed eerily quiet. Unusually quiet compared to the last couple of days.

Aunt Ruth and Raven were engrossed in conversation at Raven's desk in the dining room when I entered.

'I cooked a fish bake tonight,' Raven said flatly. 'There's plenty left. It's in the fridge if you're hungry.'

'Thanks,' I said as I took a seat. 'How was your day? It looks like it didn't go too well.'

His mouth turned down, and he sighed. 'Not great.'

Aunt Ruth looked away. 'Festering boils and bubbling pustules!' she declared with a slight huff.

My eyes widened. What had occurred to upset them both? 'What happened?' I whispered.

Raven leaned forward, gripping the edges of his chair, and opened his mouth to explain.

'The warlock's gone,' Aunt Ruth interjected before he could begin.

'Gone?' I gasped, taken aback. 'Why?'

'We had an argument with him after he hit Zara,' Raven said with obvious agitation in his voice. 'We told him that was unacceptable and he had to leave.'

My heart sank, appalled at this news. 'He hit her?' I asked indignantly.

Aunt Ruth nodded sadly while Raven gritted his teeth, obviously still angry over the matter. 'To be precise,' she began slowly, choosing her words carefully, 'when we found them, he was sitting on the sofa while his walking cane chased poor Zara around the room, whacking her.'

My stomach churned. 'But why would he do such a thing?' I asked incredulously.

Raven shook his head. 'Abaddon flew into a rage at Zara this afternoon for some reason we don't know. We heard them shouting in the living room and went to investigate. There didn't seem to be any logic to it. They were simply throwing insults at each other. And then he must have sent his walking cane after her.'

'How terrible!' I said, taking a seat.

'We argued with him for quite some time before he finally left,' Aunt Ruth said. 'He is a horribly unpleasant man. I wish we'd never called him.'

I met Aunt Ruth's gaze. 'Yes, he's not the nicest character to spend time with, I agree.'

'I think he didn't want to stay here any longer and was blaming Zara for not doing the work he sent her to do,' Raven said.

'That's no excuse to punish her like that,' Aunt Ruth said dryly. 'It's assault. We should have reported him.'

'We're not likely to see him again,' Raven added. He hung his head forlornly. 'But we still have the same problem. A shattered magic mirror.'

The mirror! I'd been so preoccupied by what Aunt Ruth and Raven had told me about the warlock's treatment of Zara, I'd forgotten why he was even here in the first place.

'I caught him copying the spell book last night,' I said. 'I made him create a copy for us too, so at least we have that.'

'The cheeky blighter,' Aunt Ruth said.

'I got the magical moissanite gem last night. He could have used it to fix the mirror today.'

'We didn't know that,' Raven muttered. He flicked his dark eyes toward me with a hint of reprimand. 'You were gone before either of us was up this morning, so we had no idea you'd been successful in your... mission.'

Dammit. My investigation on the riverbank that morning meant I left too early to hand over the precious gem to Raven or Aunt Ruth. The warlock could have repaired the mirror in the morning and perhaps avoided the fight with Zara later.

'Maybe you could have left it with a note before you went,' Aunt Ruth suggested.

'Yes, I should have done that. I'm sorry. I had something else on my mind this morning,' I said. *Fuuuuuuck.*

'But you couldn't have anticipated Abaddon would leave like that,' Raven conceded.

'He's not kept his end of the bargain,' I said. 'I should call him.'

'Tomorrow,' Aunt Ruth said. 'Let things settle a bit first.'

'All right.' I sighed. 'How is Zara after that beating? Is she okay?' Anxious, I glanced around, as if expecting her to appear any second. 'Is she here?'

'No.' Raven exhaled loudly. 'She left with the warlock.'

Chapter 19

I HEATED THE REST OF the fish bake Raven had made and plopped down at the dining room table to eat it. It had been a long day, but I still had to figure out how to move forward. Three things circled my mind like vultures as I picked at my dinner.

First, I had to make Abaddon fix the magic mirror, like he'd promised. The chance of him coming back to Kingston upon Thames to do so was extremely slim. I'd have to take the mirror to him and stay there until he'd done it. I didn't want to leave Aunt Ruth for even a couple of days, but now he'd left me no choice.

Second, I wanted to get Zara away from him, at least temporarily. Whatever she was gaining from his teachings surely wasn't worth the physical and emotional abuse he inflicted upon her.

Last, I was even more determined to puzzle out what had happened to Jane Middlemore since Lydia and I had spoken to Mr O'Grady. Had some unknown person pushed Jane into the river? I wanted to find that person, but I couldn't do everything at once. Trying to find Jane's walking companion would have to wait. Fixing Aunt Ruth's mirror had to come first.

I dialled Lydia's number.

There was a pause before she picked up the phone. The canned laughter from a sitcom abruptly cut off in the background, and I heard her voice on the other end of the line.

'Hiya, Heather. Is everything okay? It's late.'

'Hey, Lydia. Sorry for calling so late. Do you remember me telling you about my aunt's magic mirror?'

'Yes. What about it?'

I explained the deal I'd made with Abaddon and how he went back on his word.

'That's not fair,' she said, 'but how can I help? My witchy skills are no better than yours.'

'Could I take a few days off work to sort this issue out, please? I know we're short-staffed, but I really must do this for my aunt.'

Lydia was silent for a moment before saying, 'Ah, of course. I understand. You can take the time off you need. It'll be a bit tricky without you, but Penny and I will manage somehow.'

I let out a sigh of relief. 'Thanks so much, Lydia,' I said gratefully. 'I really appreciate it.'

'Text and let me know how it goes.'

'I will. Are you going to continue our investigation while I'm away?'

Lydia groaned. 'I want to, but I can't think of how to work out who Jane was with.'

'Yeah, I know. It's a blocker. Thanks for letting me have the leave.'

'No problem. Good luck.'

I ended the call, then noticed Raven standing in the doorway, his dark brown eyes sparkling with quiet enthusiasm.

'I'll go with you,' he said.

I smiled. It was tempting to have his company for the trip, but it would mean leaving Aunt Ruth on her own. 'Thanks, but I think I can carry the mirror frame by myself.'

He crossed his arms and grinned. 'Yeah, sure. But can you carry it back once it's filled with glass? It'll be much heavier then.'

Shit. No, I wouldn't be able to handle that.

'I'm happy to help you and your aunt, Heather. You know that.'

He was always so incredibly generous with his time and energy. 'I appreciate it, but I'm worried about leaving Aunt Ruth on her own if we both go. She'll have her home help during the day, but there won't be anyone here in the evenings and at night.'

'Why don't you give Pearl a call and ask her if she can stay here while we're away? I'm sure she would appreciate the extra cash.'

Of course! Why hadn't I thought of that before? 'Good idea. I'll do that.' I phoned her and explained the situation. Raven waited patiently until I hung up.

'She's willing to help,' I said, beaming at Raven. 'That woman is a goldmine of help, a real life-saver.'

He grinned. 'She sure is. Let's talk to your aunt and book some train tickets!'

WE EXPLAINED THE SITUATION to Aunt Ruth, and she agreed that Raven and I going to Abaddon's house was the best course of action. When I told her Pearl had agreed to stay with her while Raven and I were away, she was delighted.

Raven excused himself at that point, mentioning something about returning to his studies. That was his way of saying he would continue his search for a way to lift the curse that plagued him.

Aunt Ruth leaned forward in her wheelchair. 'I offered to help you with your magic when we had time, but with everything that's been going on, we haven't done it. I'd like to teach you something before you go north.'

'It'll have to be tonight because Raven and I are leaving first thing in the morning.'

'I know. It's getting late, but it's important. Let's go outside.'

I pushed her wheelchair into the hall, over the tiny ramp across the threshold and down the larger ramp to reach the front garden path, eager to learn whatever she could teach me.

'You learned the theory,' Aunt Ruth began. 'Simple spells can be cast with the magic you can summon from within. Intense spells require a source of magical power, such as—'

'A magic mirror,' I finished for her, once again experiencing a stab of guilt over breaking the damned thing.

'Yes. It could be anything. An amulet. An old vase. Something mysterious, beautiful and valuable is best.' She locked her intense gaze on mine, her eyes filled with a mysterious glint. 'After September third, you can have the magic mirror.'

That foreboding date sent a wave of despair sweeping through me. 'Oh, Aunt Ruth! What is it about that precise date that makes you think you won't survive it?'

'Never you mind about it right now. Keep focused on this task. All right?'

My heart raced as I considered her premonition—or whatever it was. Every time either Raven or I had tried to bring up the subject, she'd avoided it, either pretending to be lost in thought or changing the subject.

'Heather, I need you to concentrate here,' Aunt Ruth added, but not unkindly.

I took a deep breath of the cool evening air and steeled myself for whatever came next. 'I'll try,' I replied. 'I've got a question: what's the difference between a simple spell and an intense spell?'

'An intense spell is merely one that you cannot cast with your own summoned magic. Usually, it requires an incantation or proximity to your magic source.'

Tilting my head in thought, I paused for a moment before replying. 'Ahh, okay.' It kind of made sense.

'All right.' Aunt Ruth slid into her role of mentor with ease, clasping her hands together in front of her lap. 'Your test indicated you have a special affinity for weather control magic. But before we get to that, we need to work on summoning your own magic.'

I sighed softly, dejected. 'The textbook made it sound easy, but I've tried by myself, and nothing happened.'

Aunt Ruth chuckled. 'Don't worry about that, Heather. Everyone has trouble summoning their magic at first. There's a simple trick to it.'

'Great,' I said eagerly. 'What's the trick?'

'You know that annoying voice inside your head that never seems to shut up?'

'I think I know what you mean,' I replied. What was it called again? Some psychological whatsit. Rose would know.

'Well, the secret is to turn it off completely, and then casting any spell you can summon enough magic for will be a breeze.'

I stared back blankly before finally asking, 'That sounds wonderful, but how do you actually do it?'

Aunt Ruth grinned. 'I said there was a trick. You'll actually learn it in the next part of your correspondence course, but I'll tell you now. Come closer.'

I bent down, and my aunt pulled me nearer so she could whisper a few words in my ear. My eyes widened. When she'd finished, I stood and exclaimed in disbelief, 'That's it?'

'No. That's the long version. Now, close your eyes and take a few minutes to get into the right state of mind. Sit on the porch if you want to.'

I followed her instructions. After a few minutes of deep breathing and reflection, I nodded.

'Make a simple hand movement,' Aunt Ruth said. 'Something you wouldn't normally do, but which you won't forget. Many witches touch their thumb to the tip of their ring finger—like this.' She demonstrated the movement for me and held the pose, waiting for me to look and imitate it. 'Close your eyes again, and focus on that symbol while using your breath to settle further into a meditative state.'

I did as she said, willing my mind to stillness until my breathing was soft and even.

'Whenever you make that hand movement from now on, your mind will automatically jump to the mental state required for spellcasting. Do you understand?' Aunt Ruth said, her voice smooth and assured.

I nodded again, wanting desperately to believe this was true. And if it was, that I wouldn't foul it up.

'Excellent! Open your eyes, Heather. Let's give it a try.'

My aunt smiled broadly as I opened my eyes, feeling pleasantly lighter and calmer than before.

'Now, let's start with the weather spells,' Aunt Ruth said. She pointed out the peonies near our porch in desperate need of watering. 'See if you can produce a tiny raincloud and water them. All you have to do is quiet that irritating part of your mind and focus on what you want to occur. If your personal magic is strong enough, it'll happen.'

The peonies occupied part of a flower bed near the porch. I stared at them, suddenly full of doubt. Did my aunt really expect me to summon rain from nowhere and water them? Was such a thing actually possible?

'Go on,' she encouraged. 'Don't forget your hand movement.'

I closed my eyes and imagined a tiny raincloud hovering above the garden and dropping rain neatly on the plants. In my mind, it was almost comical, like something I might see in an old cartoon. Yet within mere seconds, the unmistakable patter of rain on plants reached my ears.

Was it coincidence? I opened my eyes. Unbelievably, a small raincloud, precisely the size of the flower bed, was drizzling rain on the thirsty peonies.

Even Aunt Ruth appeared incredulous. 'That's the best first effort I've ever seen,' she said.

I was speechless. I hadn't expected success like that either.

'Okay, try creating a breeze. Make the wind chimes tinkle.'

I turned my attention to them. This time, I kept my eyes open while I imagined a light wind.

The chimes clanged together as if in a fierce wind, though I couldn't detect even the slightest breeze. After a few seconds of intense jangling, the chimes tore free from their mooring hanging from the porch roof and flew off into the night sky like bits of confetti in a gale.

Aunt Ruth let out a huge breath. 'You've got the talent, Heather—now you only need to work on controlling it better.'

'I can see that. Sorry about the wind chimes.'

'It's late. Let's leave the lessons for now.'

I wheeled her inside, taking a quick glance over my shoulder. The miniature raincloud had vanished, and the flowers were dripping water.

Oh, was I going to have some fun with this weather magic!

Chapter 20

RAVEN AND I REACHED Abaddon's mansion in Berwick upon Tweed in the evening of the following day. It stood tall on a hill overlooking the town, its walls and dark spires blocking the night sky like an oppressive shadow. Thick iron fences surrounded the grounds. They were topped with sharp spikes that glinted in the low sunlight.

The gate was unlocked. A driveway led up to a grand entrance flanked by two tall towers.

The mansion's stone walls were carved with intricate faces of angels and demons (mostly the latter, from what I could see). Its windows were filled with stained glass that seeped a red light onto the rough cobblestone path below. A chill in the air and a sense of dread made me shiver involuntarily.

Our taxi stopped outside the entrance. The driver's agitation gave the impression that he wanted to leave the place quickly.

Raven hoisted the mirror frame out of the taxi while I paid the driver. He carried it to the porch, where he leaned it against the wall of the house. I joined him and stood before the towering front doors of Abaddon's house, fists clenched, and pounded upon the solid wood with all the fury of a storm.

The glass in the door's windowpanes flashed in the light of the setting sun, a reminder of the magical sorceries Abaddon was apparently famous for. He was in no hurry to answer my knock.

'Abaddon!' I called. 'Are you in there? We're not leaving!'

I'd wait out the whole night if I had to, but finally, the door creaked open.

'About time,' Raven muttered, crossing his arms with an expectant look on his face.

Abaddon stood on the other side of the door, tall and imposing, his eyes dark and intense. He wore a robe of midnight velvet, and his hair cascaded down in long black locks like a storm cloud. He leaned on his walking cane.

'What is it you wish from me, Heather?' he asked, his voice a deep rumble. Then he saw Raven with the mirror propped up against the side of his house. 'I see,' he added drolly.

I squared my shoulders, determined not to be intimidated by the warlock. 'You promised to repair the magic mirror, but you left without doing so. We got you everything you asked for: the plants and the gem. And you copied the spell book. You made no effort to keep your word.'

Raven took a step closer, his jaw set, backing me up.

Abaddon snapped and gestured at Raven. 'He and your moody aunt told me to leave!'

'What I said was you should leave immediately after repairing the mirror,' Raven said. 'You were hitting Zara.'

'I was not. Anyway, it was a personal matter between her and me.' Abaddon sniffed, his nostrils flaring. 'It was nothing to do with you.'

I stepped toward him, my voice rising with anger. 'It has everything to do with us if it happens in our house. And, by the way, where is Zara?'

'Oh, she's around here somewhere.' He turned and called into the house. 'Zara, come here for a minute, would you?'

We waited on the porch in the cool night air, waiting for Zara to appear. After a few moments of silence, she came into view. She was careful to keep her distance from Abaddon as she approached the door, her expression grim.

'Hello there, Zara!' I said brightly to lighten the mood. 'How are you?'

She didn't seem to be in the mood for pleasantries, though, and only blinked in response.

'Are you okay?' Raven asked cautiously, his gaze intently focused on her.

She gave a curt nod.

'Good,' I said, trying to determine if she was being truthful or hiding something. It was impossible to tell from her minimal body language.

'Can we come in?' Raven asked, lifting the mirror frame as if we'd already been invited in.

'Of course,' the warlock replied dryly and moved aside.

We entered, Raven bringing the mirror frame through like it weighed nothing at all. The door closed behind us of its own accord with an eerie echo that sent shivers down my spine.

'We'll stay only long enough for you to repair this,' Raven said in a gruff tone as we bustled inside. 'Then we'll depart.'

'I brought the magical moissanite gem with me,' I said.

'Excellent,' Abaddon said, 'but I insist you stay the night. I have plenty of rooms. Repairing the mirror is a lengthy task, in any case. I cannot rush it.'

I glanced at Raven, who shrugged. 'All right,' I said.

'Follow me,' the warlock said before leading us down the wide hallway and into a vast chamber. We gazed around in awe. A fire crackled in a hearth, and glittering crystals dangled from the ceiling, sending glimmering lights dancing over the walls. Everywhere I looked, peculiar artefacts and arcane trinkets of all shapes and sizes filled the shelves and tables. Some of them hummed softly with magical power. This was the home of a formidable warlock, all right. One who could weave powerful spells.

'Leave the mirror frame there,' Abaddon commanded, pointing to an empty table, 'and give me the magical gem. I will restore the magic mirror tonight.'

'I want to watch,' I said, setting my feet.

Abaddon gave an indifferent shrug. 'As you wish. Zara, arrange some food for everyone, and show the birdman to a room where he can rest or sleep.'

'I will stay here with Heather,' Raven said in a tone that brooked no argument. Neither of us intended to leave Abaddon's presence until he'd kept his promise to fix the magic mirror.

Zara left us, presumably to see to preparing dinner.

Abaddon glared at Raven for a moment, his eyebrows drawn together in a deep scowl, but said nothing more to him. He shifted his attention to me and extended an open hand, palm up.

'I will need the gemstone,' he demanded.

My heart thumping, I dug into my handbag, unzipped an inside pocket and pulled it out. In the flickering light from the fire, the moissanite gem sparkled and shone with multicoloured brilliance that contrasted with Abaddon's dark presence. I pressed it into his hand, relieved that, at last, he had what he needed to fix the magic mirror.

The warlock scrutinised it before turning back to me, expressionless. 'This is the exact gemstone I mentioned. Now, tell me how you obtained it... and do not lie to me.'

I glanced between Abaddon and Raven, who remained silent but equally interested in my response. Taking a deep breath, I admitted in a hushed voice, 'I, uh, stole it. But I will pay for it. I already got a valuation from a jeweller's shop in Kingston.'

'That would be the value of the gem, but not of the magic,' the warlock said.

A wave of frustration hit me. 'I know, but the witch who owned it passed away recently. I couldn't wait months to negotiate with her heirs. My aunt needs her magic mirror back, so she can cast a healing spell—'

Abaddon dismissed my words with a wave of his hand and looked away. 'You've told me all that already.' He sighed impatiently, peering into the flames as if seeking answers there instead. 'She manages perfectly well. It's not as if she has a life-threatening illness.'

'It's more complicated than that,' Raven said. 'She's told us she has less than three months to live, without explaining how she knows that. We hope that powerful spells she could cast using the mirror's magic might help her.'

The warlock faced Raven. His whole demeanour altered. 'I didn't know. You should have told me.' The haughtiness had gone from his voice.

'Would it have made a difference?' Raven said acerbically.

'Yes. I would not have allowed you to drive me away before I'd fixed the mirror. I am always kind to people in genuine need.'

'But you hit your assistant with a stick!' Raven blurted out.

Abaddon drew back and raised an eyebrow in surprise. 'Did you actually see me hit her with a stick?'

'No, but it was your magic that powered the stick to do it.'

Abaddon stroked his chin. 'Was it? You're blaming me?'

'That's quite enough, you two,' I snapped. 'We didn't come here to start another fight. We only want the mirror fixed.'

'Of course.'

At that moment, Zara poked her head into the room and announced brightly, 'Dinner will be served in the dining room in five minutes!'

'Excellent,' Abaddon replied. 'Let's eat, and then I will fix the mirror. Zara, lead the way to the dining room, if you would, please.'

We followed her across the wide hallway and down another passage before emerging into a large dining room that reminded me of a great hall in an old castle. The flagstone floor did not appear to be ancient, though, but the walls were decorated with massive colourful tapestries, which did look the worse for age. There was even a dented suit of armour standing in one corner.

Abaddon bade us to sit. He took one end of the table, while the rest of us spread along one side, Zara being the farthest away from him.

Dinner conversation with Abaddon at Aunt Ruth's house had almost put me off my food. He'd been rude and taciturn. Would tonight's meal be any different?

Raven chatted to Zara about something. I took out my phone. Did I have time to send a quick text to Rachel? Maybe. I started tapping.

But before I could even type out 'hey there', the door flew open, and an elderly lady wearing a chef's hat wheeled a wooden trolley into the room. Four covered plates sat on top of the trolley.

The lady seemed sprightly for her age. Perhaps she was one of those people who never retire because they feel they must keep working. But she didn't look happy—far from it. Her expression was one of abject misery.

She strode to the dining room table, her ancient joints creaking as she placed a plate in front of each of us with an almost magical steadiness before she finally spoke.

'I didna know ye was expecting visitors, Mr Masana,' she said with a thick Scottish lilt. 'Ye could've given me a bit o' warning, at least. I had tae rush around like a lunatic and throw something together.' She sighed and brushed off her apron as if clearing away a layer of flour. 'It's not much, mind ye, nae near enough fer a proper dinner.'

Abaddon gave what was seemingly meant to be a reassuring smile. 'I'm sure it will be perfectly adequate, Mrs Brown. Thank you for your last-minute efforts.'

The old woman's joints groaned as she turned towards him with one doubtful eyebrow raised. 'Aye, well, I suppose I'll have tae make an extra big pot o' porridge fer yer breakfast, too?'

'Again, thank you,' Abaddon said.

With that, the old cook turned and pushed the trolley from the room.

I lifted the lid off my plate, with butterflies in my stomach. What kind of culinary delights would a warlock's elderly cook prepare for him and his uninvited guests?

The dish was roasted venison with rosemary and garlic, and it was fantastic. Truly delicious. Maybe the cook was a witch herself, specialising in cooking spells?

Once the meal was over, thankfully with a minimum of terse exchanges and arguments, Abaddon asked us to return to the room where we had left the magic mirror on a large table. The fire still burned brightly in the hearth, as if someone had added more wood.

A frisson of excitement and apprehension surged through me as I anticipated the warlock performing the magic spell we'd all waited for.

Abaddon gestured for us to step back from the mirror to give him space. He paced back and forth, relying on his cane for support—the same cane that had beaten Zara—apparently deliberating how to begin.

This persisted for several minutes.

Raven glanced at me with raised eyebrows and mouthed, 'What's going on?'

I shrugged and tried to make eye contact with Zara, who wouldn't meet my gaze.

A SPELL OF MIRROR MAGIC

At long last, Abaddon stopped abruptly and placed one hand on the mirror frame. He lifted his head and stared at us.

'I can't do it,' he said.

Chapter 21

MY STOMACH CLENCHED so hard it sent a shot of pain through me. 'What do you mean, you can't do it?' I cried, my voice echoing off the walls.

Raven remained calm and composed, even though he must be seething inside. 'Would you care to explain, Abaddon?'

The warlock slumped into a chair. He clasped his hands in his lap and fixed us with an intense gaze. 'To properly mend this mirror, something extra is needed.'

My stomach dropped. *Fuck. Not again.* 'What now?' I demanded. 'You can't keep changing the deal on us!'

He shook his head slowly with a heavy sigh. 'I'm not attempting to extort any more payment from you. I'm merely endeavouring to create the environment in which my spell will succeed.'

'And that is?' Raven asked, his forehead creasing.

Abaddon lifted his face towards the ceiling dramatically and declared, 'This intricate piece of magic requires positive emotions if it is to succeed. Unfortunately, I'm too drained and jaded to summon the required magical energy right now. I'm more than a little sad—quite depressed, to be precise.' His arms opened wide in an exaggerated gesture that seemed almost comical, given our circumstances. 'The spell cannot work while I am in this state of mind.'

Raven face-palmed. Zara squirmed in her seat, perhaps thinking she might later be blamed for this.

I took a deep breath and tried my best to keep my frustration at bay before speaking. 'Let me understand this,' I began cautiously. 'You're unhappy and that's preventing you from meeting your side of the deal—even though you've already taken what you wanted as payment?'

Abaddon glared at Zara before his eyes bored into me. 'It's far more complicated than that.' He sighed. 'I need to infuse the mirror with positive energy. Without that, it will not work.'

'Couldn't you have told us that sooner?' I snapped.

Raven glared. 'Okay. Let's try to move forward. What do we need to do to help you be emotionally prepared for casting the spell?'

The warlock raised a pointed finger. 'I know the exact thing.'

Oh great. He better not want sex or something weird like that. If he is going to ask for something strange, we'll find someone else to do the job instead.

Abaddon continued. 'It is something priceless, yet free... perhaps difficult to find.'

'That's a riddle,' Raven muttered.

'It's too vague,' I said, looking around as if the answer might magically present itself. 'I don't have the faintest idea what you mean.'

'I'll try to explain.' Abaddon lowered his head. He seemed to sag, the aloofness and superciliousness leaving him for now. 'No one is perfect. Not even me.'

That's certainly true.

'There are times when an individual may act badly. Perhaps they make mistakes—big mistakes—ones that might hurt someone else, even someone who is important to them.' Abaddon glanced at Zara once more.

Raven and I exchanged another glance. He was referring to beating his assistant, wasn't he? Is the warlock remorseful? Does he seek redemption?

'What I mean,' he continued, 'is that sometimes it is necessary to ask for, or to grant, forgiveness for some dark deed. But my question is... how does one do this?'

'You want to know how forgiveness works? Is that it?' I asked incredulously. It was like I was in a psychology class instead of attempting to have Aunt Ruth's magic mirror fixed.

Abaddon nodded slowly. 'Not only how it works, but what must be done, or said, to make it happen.' His gaze met mine with a deep expression of sadness.

Raven coughed politely, cutting through the tension. 'Well, I think the first step is to admit to the wrong that was done and to express regret or remorse. Then, it's important to be open and honest about what happened, and to make a commitment to never repeat the same mistake. The other person may also need some sort of recompense, such as an apology, a gesture of reparation or simply a promise to make things right.'

Abaddon pondered this for a moment before replying. 'Yes, that might do it.'

I breathed a sigh of relief that we hadn't reached an impasse. 'Well, I suppose we should get started.'

'Excellent,' the warlock said. 'I'm sure it won't be too difficult to find a forgiveness spell or potion, even here in Berwick upon Tweed.'

I inwardly groaned. 'No, that's not how it works. You can't find true forgiveness with a potion. It has to come from the heart.'

'The heart?' Abaddon's brow wrinkled while he contemplated this. 'I see... so that will generate positive emotional energy?'

I bit back my sharp retort. Was he being deliberately obtuse, or was he at the lower end of the emotional IQ scale?

'So, forgiveness involves both the perpetrator and the victim, correct?' the warlock said.

'That's how I see it,' Raven said, observing Abaddon, 'though other people may think differently. To my mind, the victim has to feel that the perpetrator of the dark deed, as you put it, regrets it.'

'And what if that is impossible?'

Raven opened his mouth and closed it again, searching for an answer that wasn't there. 'I'm not sure,' he conceded with a groan.

The warlock turned to me with a hopeful gleam in his eye. 'Do you know?'

'No, I can't give you the answer you need. I don't really understand what you want, Abaddon.'

Zara was curled up in her chair, as if trying to disappear. What had he done to the poor girl for her to shrink back so far into herself?

Raven's eyes lit up. 'I think I understand. You're asking us to help you repair your relationship with Zara.'

I had guessed that, but my curiosity was calling, *Details! Details!*

'Yes. That's correct.' Abaddon grimaced and shook his head as if to clear it of unwanted thoughts. 'This is new to me. Until recently, I could summon the magic I required because I was of sound mind and possessed a positive outlook.'

A positive outlook? Is that how he saw himself? Really?

'But now, there is an emotional barrier blocking my expression of my most powerful sorceries.'

'And you can't fix the magic mirror until we help you remove this emotional barrier,' Raven concluded flatly.

Abaddon nodded vigorously and tapped the side of his head. 'Exactly. As I said, I've never had this state-of-mind issue before.' He glanced between Raven and me expectantly, and we both stared at him blankly—clearly, he was expecting us to solve this problem for him!

After an awkward silence, he gestured wildly with his hands. 'Tomorrow, maybe you could pop down to the apothecary in the town and see if they have a suitable elixir?'

Now it was my turn to facepalm. He just didn't get it.

CLEARLY, WE WOULD NOT achieve anything more that night. Abaddon had suggested we stay, and Zara—uncharacteristically quiet—showed us to our rooms.

Mine was huge and furnished with antiques and a four-poster bed similar to those at Chirtlewood. The walls were made of brightly polished, golden-coloured wood that was not painted but stained. It was deathly quiet. I half-expected a ghost to pop up out of nowhere.

It was the middle of the evening—too early for me to go to bed. But Aunt Ruth might have, so I sent a text instead of phoning.

Hi. We've arrived. Abaddon couldn't fix the mirror on his first attempt. Don't worry. Raven and I will get him the help he needs to complete the job. We might be away an extra day or two, though.

I read on my phone for a few minutes, waiting to see if Aunt Ruth would reply. She didn't. She must have gone to sleep already.

It was a perfect time to call New Zealand, though. Rose should be awake by now. I video called her.

She answered almost immediately. Her face sprang onto the screen. She had a half-eaten piece of buttered toast in one hand and waved to me with the other, her mouth full. In the background, a young woman poured water from a steaming kettle into a mug with an owl on it.

'Hi, Rose,' I said brightly. 'How's everything? I hope you sorted out that issue with your dad. It was quite inconsiderate of him to insist on staying with you when all you have is a measly room in a shared student flat. I suppose it wasn't a surprise, though. Typical! He always did think too much of himself.'

Rose's eyes widened, and she made a frantic gesture while she desperately gulped down her toast before responding. 'Mum—' she squeaked.

Before she could finish, Terry leaned into view, wearing a white singlet, partially obscuring my view of Rose. He had a steaming cup in one hand. 'Hi, Heather. How nice it is to see you,' he said. His tone dripped with sarcasm so thick you could practically see it oozing off him like golden syrup.

I frowned. 'What are you doing at Rose's place at eight in the morning, half-dressed?' I asked, eyeing him with suspicion.

He shrugged nonchalantly while still smirking, as if he had secretly won lotto. 'I'm staying here while I sort my shit out. Didn't she tell you?'

'You've got enough money to pay for your own place,' I asserted, trying my best to sound reasonable. 'Don't be a burden on our daughter.'

'Mum, it'll be okay,' Rose interjected, her voice shaking. 'It's only for a week or two.'

'Why doesn't he stay in a hotel like normal people?' I retorted, feeling the tension rise.

'It'll be a month at the most,' Terry added. 'Maybe two, but who's counting? Besides, while I'm here, I can help Rose with her studies.'

'You studied accounting, Terry. You know nothing about psychology,' I reminded him, exasperated.

He waved my objections away with a flourish of his hand. 'Yeah, but psychology is just common sense, isn't it? Besides, I have life experience.'

Rose rolled her eyes in disbelief.

I fumed at his ignorance. 'Do you mind if I speak with my daughter alone?'

One side of his mouth turned down in annoyance. 'Sure. I was about to go to my room, anyway.' He disappeared from the screen, and Rose came back into full focus.

'Sorry about that,' she said.

'I'm confused. I thought you were going to tell him he couldn't stay with you.'

'Yes, but he didn't give me any choice. He turned up on the doorstep at ten o'clock one night.'

'Where's he sleeping? On the floor in your room?'

'Actually...' Rose hesitated. Her cheeks reddened and her gaze flicked to the side. 'He's sleeping in the bed.'

My stomach lurched. 'What? That's... You mean you're sleeping on the floor in your own room?'

'Oh, no. I'm squeezing in with Madison.' She looked to the side. 'Hey, Maddie, say hello to my mum.'

The angle of the camera shifted, making it seem like I was hurtling through Rose's kitchen at an inconceivable speed. I blinked. When I opened my eyes again, a young woman with a nose ring and wild green streaks in her hair was smiling at me from the other side of the screen.

'Hi, I'm Maddie,' she said cheerfully.

'Hi.' I returned the smile. 'You're one of Rose's flatmates, then? What are you studying?'

Maddie grinned. 'I was studying fine arts, but I dropped out to work on my art full time.'

'I love art. I plan to visit some of the major galleries in London soon. What kind of art do you make?'

'I paint teacups—like, real-life ones—then I smash them up and glue them back together in stacks!' She squealed with delight. 'It's so cool.'

'That sounds... creative.' I couldn't help but chuckle at the absurdity of it all. 'Maybe Rose could send me a photo of your work, if you don't mind.'

'Not at all!' Maddie beamed at me.

'It's very kind of you to let Rose share your room while her dad stays.'

Maddie giggled, revealing a row of perfect white teeth. 'Honestly, it's a pleasure.' She passed the phone back.

Rose appeared again. 'Hi, Mum. Look...' She bit her lip.

'Do you want me to tell Terry to move out? Your dad should easily find a flat for himself. I understand if you're finding it hard to handle the situation yourself. He's so inconsiderate that he wouldn't think of taking your needs into account.'

Rose shook her head, her face lighting with a smile. 'It's not that. I wanted to tell you that Maddie and I are together.'

I paused, my heart rate speeding up in surprise. 'You mean... together, together?'

'Yes! We connect really well, and I've never been happier!'

'That's wonderful, Rose! Congratulations,' I said warmly.

'Thanks, Mum. I better go. I've got to get ready.'

'Sure. It's getting late here, anyway.'

We disconnected. I plonked onto the bed. What effect would the young woman who breaks teacups and glues them back together have on my daughter?

Chapter 22

ZARA BROUGHT ME AN overloaded breakfast tray in the morning at about eight o'clock. The aroma of apple juice, steaming porridge topped with brown sugar, a stack of buttered toast and freshly brewed coffee was heavenly. I still hadn't got out of bed.

'Good morning, Zara. This looks wonderful! Thank you very much.' I took the tray from her.

'Oh, I didn't make it. That was Mrs Brown. She's such a sweetie. I only brought it to you.'

'That was very thoughtful of you both.'

'Thanks.'

'How are you this morning?' I asked, noticing how tired she looked.

'I'm exhausted,' she said with a yawn. 'I didn't sleep well. And I haven't eaten yet.'

'Why did you have trouble sleeping?' I prodded gently.

Zara sighed and looked away. 'I was thinking about Abaddon and his request. I know he needs help, but I'm not sure what I can do.'

I couldn't tell if she was being cautious or just didn't want to talk about it—so I tried to lighten the mood.

'Well, whatever it is, we'll figure it out together—but for now, why don't you relax and go and have some breakfast?'

She smiled weakly and nodded. 'Yes, that's a good idea.'

THE BREAKFAST WAS DELICIOUS. After eating, I got dressed, and then my phone rang with an incoming video call. Rachel.

I answered with a smile. 'Hey there. How are things with you?'

Rachel sighed and stuck out her bottom lip in an exaggerated pout. That could mean only one thing.

'Did you break up with Rick?' I asked, already knowing the answer.

'He broke up with me, actually.'

'Oh, Rach, that stinks. You said things were going so well the last time we talked. What happened?'

'Well... you know how I was worried he might be trying to spy on my firm and get inside info on my big case?'

'I remember.' I slipped my shoes on and stood. 'Did you confront him about it?'

'Um... not exactly.'

'What went wrong, then?'

'I stayed over at his flat after our last date. He has this really cool apartment overlooking Hagley Park. Private balcony, all mod cons, everything. Must be worth a million at least.'

'Uh-huh. So, what happened? You're avoiding the question.'

Rachel sighed, rubbing her face in resignation. 'Right. Yes. Well, I was worried about his motives, as you know, so when he took a shower, I rifled through his briefcase, looking for anything to confirm my suspicions. Bad idea!'

I raised an eyebrow at this. 'And he caught you in the act, right?'

Rachel groaned. 'You got it. He wasn't impressed. So, he broke up with me there and then.'

I avoided pointing out the irony in the situation. My bestie would be well aware of it herself. 'I'm sorry to hear that, Rach.'

'Yeah, well, *mea culpa*. I fucked up. But that's enough about me. I was calling to check on you, girlfriend. When we last spoke, you didn't seem like yourself. I know something was troubling you. Want to talk about it yet?'

I'd expected this. Rachel and I had been best friends for so long that she could practically read my mind. She couldn't guess the problem, but she knew it was eating at me, and she wouldn't let up until she found out the truth.

How could I even explain my new life of magic and ghosts? My tongue was heavy in my mouth, and I forced myself to say, 'Um, not yet. Soon.' How long could I put this off?

'Hey, that's not your aunt's house, is it? You've got a four-poster bed. That's cool.'

I laughed. 'I'm having a few days away. I'm up north, near the Scottish border.'

'Awesome. That must be nice. And now it's you avoiding the question.'

Ever the lawyer. 'It's really complicated, Rach. I'm not even sure how to explain it all, or if you will even believe me.'

'Is it to do with your not-yet-boyfriend?'

'Partly, yes. But I'm also worried about my aunt's health, and—' And what? Wayward magic? A death premonition? Finishing my witchcraft assignments?

'I'm here for you,' Rachel said gently. 'We can talk it through like we always do. That's what besties are for, isn't it?'

Her words made some of my fear subside and I managed a small smile in reply. 'Yes, of course. Okay, I'll talk with you real soon. I promise. But first, let me figure out how to explain it all.'

Rachel looked bemused. 'Fine. You can put me off again, but please remember I want to help.'

'I know. Thanks, Rach.' A knock came at my door. It was probably Raven. 'I've gotta go. Let's talk soon, okay?'

'You can count on it.'

FOLLOWING BREAKFAST, Raven and I strolled towards the apothecary in the town centre, a mission that seemed doomed from the start. We both knew Abaddon's request for a potion to produce forgiveness was ridiculous, but until we thought of something better, it seemed as good a plan as any.

The owner of the apothecary, an old woman with wispy white hair and worn eyes, listened to our request and then cackled with laughter.

'You two want a forgiveness potion? Ha! That's quite impossible, I'm afraid. Forgiveness isn't something you can mix up in a bottle. It takes patience, understanding, and plenty of time.'

'Yeah, we know,' I said, 'but a warlock told us to come here and ask for one.'

'Even though we told him no such thing exists,' Raven added.

'Do you mean the warlock who lives in the mansion on the hill?'

'Yes, that's him,' I said.

The shopkeeper scratched her nose and frowned. 'He's a loner. Quite strange. Perhaps he's a little odd in the head to ask for such things.'

'Thanks for confirming what we thought,' Raven said.

We left the apothecary and wandered along the cobbled streets until we found a quaint café. Once inside, I ordered a white hot chocolate, and Raven asked for a cappuccino. We took a seat at the window, and once our drinks arrived, we discussed our puzzling situation with Abaddon.

'What the hell do you think is going on with him?' Raven asked, his brows furrowed in frustration. He took a sip of his coffee. 'I can't figure it out. Why doesn't Abaddon simply apologise to Zara and ask her to forgive him? Or ask what he can do to make things right?'

I shrugged, also frustrated. 'There must be more to this than we know, but they aren't likely to talk about it in front of us. Unless... do you think there's a chance we may have misunderstood something or jumped to conclusions that aren't true?'

Raven shook his head and put his cup down. 'I don't think so. Maybe we should try talking to them separately. I could have a chat with Abaddon, and you could see if Zara would open up to you. Back home, she appeared to warm to you a bit more than to me.'

'Good idea. Let's try that. We might get somewhere. If not, I don't know what we'll do.'

Raven reached over the table and took my hand in his, giving it a comforting squeeze before releasing it again. He was being supportive rather than trying to be romantic, but, even so, a small thrill went through me. I let my mind wander off to daydreams of long weekends spent together in charming little villages—only to realise that if I was to share my thoughts it would probably trigger Raven's curse...

'We'll find a way somehow,' he whispered, trying to comfort me, despite our quandary. 'Try not to worry.'

Worrying was something I did far too much of, and Raven knew it.

'Thanks,' I sighed. 'Shall we have another drink before we head back? It's on me this time.'

IT WAS LATE MORNING when Raven and I arrived back at Abaddon's mansion with renewed hope that we might find a way through the impasse. Once there, we parted ways. Raven scurried off in search of the warlock, and I went to look for Zara.

I found her in one of the two libraries, sorting through a pile of scrolls on a table.

'Can I help you, Heather?' she asked when I entered.

I marvelled at the room's contents. This library was the smaller of the two. Giant leather-bound books about magic, astronomy, astrology, supernatural creatures and more were shelved alongside curious artefacts whose purpose I didn't recognise. It had the faint scent of musty books, dusty shelves and old parchments.

I sauntered over and made myself comfortable in a leather chair opposite Zara, my palms sweating as I tried to phrase my question delicately. 'You know how important it is that Abaddon fixes the magic mirror for us, don't you, Zara? My aunt needs it.'

Zara lifted her head and met my gaze. 'I know.'

I measured my next words carefully. 'What is the problem between you and Abaddon?' I asked carefully. 'The beating? Anything else?'

Her gaze hardened. 'What makes you assume there's a problem? And why would it be any of your business, anyway?' Her words vibrated throughout the library like a distant thunder.

I nodded, resigned. 'Okay... I understand. I only want you to know that I'm here if you need me.'

'Until you return to Kingston upon Thames,' Zara snapped.

'Yes, that's true, but I'm available to talk to you while I'm here if it would help.'

Zara's face softened a little. 'Thank you,' she said, her voice barely above a whisper.

We sat in silence for a few moments before Zara spoke again. 'It's complicated,' she said. 'The warlock treats me like crap sometimes...' Her gaze shifted away from mine as her voice faded. 'I don't want to talk about it.'

I nodded, understanding her need for privacy, though my mind was spinning with questions. 'I won't pry. But I do remember what it was like to be young and misunderstood. If you ever need to get away, call me.'

She smiled gratefully, and we sat together in companionable silence for a few moments more. Then, with a sigh, she returned her attention to the scrolls.

I left her to it, knowing that I had done what I could. I had offered a listening ear and a supportive presence, but she hadn't opened up to me. I was no closer to resolving the problem between her and Abaddon, and I feared that meant he still could not summon the magic he needed to help us.

As I headed out into the gardens of the mansion, I could only hope that Raven had had more success than me.

Chapter 23

I FOUND RAVEN ALREADY sitting at the foot of the fountain we'd arranged to meet at. He glanced up glumly as I approached.

I lowered myself to the stone slab next to him. 'You got nowhere either, I guess?'

'He told me it was far too sensitive a matter for him to explain, said it was none of my business and called me a fool when I offered to help anyway.'

'Did it seem like he was in the right frame of mind to fix the mirror?'

Raven shook his head and sighed. 'If anything, he appeared even more upset than last night.'

'Maybe we should find another warlock or witch to help us?'

He crossed his arms and frowned, deep in thought. 'That would put us back at square one. We'd need to find someone, negotiate payment—' He waved off the rest of his sentence with a flick of his fingers. 'You know.'

'So... what do you want to do now?'

Raven considered it for a minute. 'How about we walk back into town and get another coffee?' He lowered his voice to a whisper. 'We can strategise away from prying ears—and eyes.' He peered around the garden apprehensively.

Were we being watched? I shivered at the thought of unseen powers nearby. Who knew what might be listening in a warlock's garden?

'Okay, I'm up for another walk and a drink.'

We strolled into the town again. It was a pleasant walk. The day was gloomy, though, which matched my sombre mood, something that coincided more and more lately. And my left knee was aching from walking on all those uneven cobblestones. My old tennis injury had never properly healed.

'How about we have lunch?' I suggested as we walked up to the same cosy café we'd visited earlier.

'Good idea.'

A few minutes later, we were seated at a window table and had placed our orders for beef stew with neeps and tatties for me and a toasted sandwich with all the fillings they had on offer for Raven. The server explained to me what 'neeps' and 'tatties' were—turnips and potatoes—and I smiled appreciatively.

'I know what Abaddon needs,' I said, breaking the suspenseful silence that had settled between us. 'Abaddon wants a quick fix for his negative emotions. Let's give him one.'

Raven frowned at me. 'Yes... But how? We both agreed there is no such thing as a potion of forgiveness.'

I grinned as the plan unfolded in my mind. 'What if we give him one, anyway? We could give him a vial of apple juice and tell him it's a potion of forgiveness—he won't be any wiser!'

I saw understanding creep into Raven's expression. 'You're talking about a placebo, like a sugar pill instead of medication. Yes, it could work, except he might be suspicious of any potion we give him because we told him that no such potion exists.'

My brain whirred as I considered alternatives to keep my plan afloat. 'Then we could give him something else instead, like an amulet.'

'Sure! Something like that might do the trick.'

I grinned. 'Let's get a suitable amulet and tell him it will promote forgiveness and dispel his negative emotions. We'll go back to Abaddon and present it to him. He'll feel better about himself because he believes we are giving him a magical solution—exactly what he asked for.'

Raven smiled. 'That sounds like a plan. What should the amulet look like?'

We chatted more about the prospective amulet and settled on finding a pendant with a gemstone that would make Abaddon feel more empowered and less anxious. With that decided, we only needed to obtain it. We paid for lunch and wandered around the quaint town, searching for a shop that might have something suitable.

Berwick upon Tweed's old town centre wasn't large, and we soon stumbled upon a crystal and gemstone store nestled between two ordinary buildings.

'This is perfect! Let's head inside!' I said, almost skipping towards the door.

A young woman with numerous tattoos and green hair down to her waist greeted us warmly with a smile. 'Welcome. How may I help you two?' she asked, her voice melodic and friendly.

'We don't know much about crystals,' I said, 'except that they are supposed to possess mystical powers. Is that true?'

The woman chuckled. 'What can I say? Some people believe in their power, and others buy them because they're pretty. What kind of crystal are you looking for, specifically?'

'A pendant for a man who is seeking forgiveness and to ease his remorse over some wrong he has committed. He hurt someone close to him.'

The saleswoman looked daggers at Raven, suspicion in her eyes.

'Oh no! I'm not the man we're talking about,' he hastily clarified. 'He's a mutual acquaintance of ours.'

'You think a crystal on a chain can absolve someone of their sins like a Catholic priest in the confessional?' she asked.

'I have no idea,' I said. 'You're the expert. You tell us.'

The woman smiled, and her eyes gleamed. 'Of course it can, if the wearer believes that it does.'

Raven nodded eagerly, as if he'd been waiting for this answer since forever. 'That's exactly what we need.'

'Fantastic. In that case, I suggest a pendant with a rose quartz gemstone.'

'Why that one?' I asked. *Is it the most expensive?*

'Its planet is Venus, and its chakra is the heart. It is said to promote self-forgiveness, bring emotional peace to its wearer and encourage harmony within relationships,' the green-haired woman explained calmly.

'That sounds like a lot from one little stone,' Raven said, frowning.

'Your mileage may vary.'

I fought back a grin. 'You said relationships. What kind?'

'Any kind. Not necessarily romantic ones. Does that suit?'

'That sounds perfect. Do you agree, Raven?'

I could see he wasn't convinced, but he gave an almost imperceptible nod. We needed something, and it may as well be this.

'We'll take it, please,' I said.

'Certainly. I'll package it for you in a gift box.'

We paid and thanked her. I tucked the small velvet gift box containing the pendant into my handbag, and we headed back towards Abaddon's mansion.

After a short while, Raven said, 'Do you think that stone will do what that woman told us it would do?'

'I guess we won't know until we try, but it doesn't actually matter what we think,' I replied. 'What matters is whether the warlock will believe it does.'

BACK AT THE MANSION, we set out to find the warlock. I imagined he was upstairs in his chambers poring over ancient manuscripts, or concocting mysterious elixirs in a cauldron. But before we even reached the front door, we spotted him meditating—or perhaps dozing—in the garden in a patch of sunlight between two manicured shrubs.

I motioned to Raven that I would stay here with him, and he mouthed to me that he would go inside.

Raven strode towards the front entrance. I'd never tire of seeing those tight butt muscles in action, but actually starting a relationship with Raven had to wait. I still had the physical twinges and fantasies of ravishment, though.

I snuck up on Abaddon—which was easier said than done with my heavy boots clicking across the flagstones like a clock tower chiming the hour until I stepped onto the grass, where my boot strikes were deadened. The lawn and garden beds were immaculately presented. Did Abaddon do his gardening using magic? I so needed a magic weeding spell.

The warlock remained completely still as I observed him. It seemed he was barely breathing. Should I wake him or let him complete his meditation or snooze undisturbed?

Perhaps I could softly call his name to alert him of my presence?

'Abaddon,' I whispered, my voice so quiet it was unfamiliar, but it caught the warlock's attention. His eyes slowly opened, and he studied me with curiosity, clearly surprised by my arrival.

'Have you found something to help me?' he asked, obviously perceiving that we had gone out searching.

I nodded and reached into my handbag to pull out the gift box with the rose quartz gemstone pendant inside. I handed it to Abaddon, who opened it. He studied it before looking up at me again with an expression of gratitude on his face.

'Thank you,' he said and placed the pendant around his neck. The weak afternoon sunlight glinted off its facets in pink flashes before he tucked it beneath his robe.

He closed his eyes again and returned to meditating or dozing—it was hard to tell which—but the air around us was calmer, as if a heavy weight had been lifted from Abaddon's shoulders, allowing him to finally find peace once more.

I sat in awe of the moment, watching him quietly. Perhaps Abaddon was incorporating the alleged powers of the pendant into his meditation right now.

As I sat there, I thought of Aunt Ruth, who must be wondering how we were doing. I made myself a silent promise to call or text her later. Although Pearl was sure to be taking excellent care of her, I should check in soon.

My thoughts drifted to Chirtlewood. I missed my job and my colleagues Lydia and Penny, even though I'd only been away for two days. A smile passed over my lips as I remembered Charlotte spooking tourists left and right and the earl tossing an invisible stick to Scruffles in the gardens. With any luck, I'd be back soon.

As for the investigation into Jane Middlemore's death... I should text the inspector about it. She might not reply, though—or she might, but only to tell me to stay out of the investigation. Maybe Lydia has followed up? I should text her too.

And Rose and Rachel. My phone would get a workout tonight.

Abaddon was so still that I wouldn't have been surprised if a bird sat on his head. How long was he going to sit there?

I stood and tiptoed away. I should tell Raven that I'd given the pendant to Abaddon, and our plan appeared to be working. Also, I wanted to talk to him about how we could help Zara.

After telling Raven that Abaddon now had the pendant and had returned to meditating, I ventured to the larger of the manor's libraries. There was nothing better to fill the time than snooping around the bookcases in someone else's house. What might a warlock read in their leisure time?

At first, it seemed a bit underwhelming. Apart from a few paperback mystery novels, there were lots of textbooks on biology and chemistry. Anatomy, especially. Hints and tips on spell-casting. The Necronomicon. An encyclopaedia of magical beasts—I flipped through the pages of that one. Several years of Scientific American. A grimoire of incantations. A treatise on dissecting amphibians. Yikes.

One wall of the room contained bookcases crammed with witchcraft tomes: the history of witchcraft, basic spells, safety for witches, and all manner of other subjects. These were much more interesting.

After browsing this sea of books for quite some time, I finally settled in an old, comfy armchair tucked away in the corner of the library. After all the walking to and from the town, I needed a rest. Then I called Aunt Ruth to update her on our progress and say we hoped to arrive home the following evening.

Chapter 24

THE SUN SLOWLY SET, the sky turning a deep tangerine before fading to the navy blue of night. I had left my meandering through the manor to find myself in the greenhouse. It was warm and humid inside, soft music was playing and, by some sort of strange magic or spell, the plants seemed to sway along with the melody. The smell of earth was pungent and sweet, like that of a freshly tilled field. The entire space was magical, as if I had strayed into a fairy tale.

The scene before me was so peaceful and surreal I remained rooted to the spot until a voice from behind me jolted me towards reality.

'There you are,' Raven chortled. 'Come inside for dinner.'

I followed him inside with a sense of anticipation gnawing at my stomach. Could the trick with the pendant have worked? Would it have improved the warlock's emotional state?

After we sat at the table, Mrs Brown entered the room with a trolley bearing four covered plates. Her mouth puckered up as if she'd forgotten to put her teeth in, and she said, 'I have grilled fish fer ye tonight with fancy tatties and mixed greens. I caught the fish meself this afternoon from my wee rowboat, half a mile offshore, so it's fresh as can be. It was the best this old woman could manage after chopping the wood and going tae the shops for supplies. I hope it's up tae scratch.'

Damn, she works so hard for an elderly servant. Or is it that everyone up here in the border territories is extremely tough?

'Thank you, Mrs Brown,' Abaddon said. 'I'm sure it will be superb, as always.'

She placed a plate in front of each of us and said, 'When ye have polished off this meagre course, I will bring in the desserts fer ye.'

'Desserts?' I said. 'Plural?'

'Bread and butter pudding, trifle and apple crumble—take yer pick or have all three.'

That's the easiest decision of the trip so far.

The fish was mouth-wateringly delicious.

As we ate, Abaddon spoke up. 'I have an announcement. I feel completely restored after my meditation earlier. Once more, thank you for the pendant. I believe it has helped considerably. When dinner is finished, I will cast the spell to repair the broken mirror, and I'm confident that this time, I can summon the necessary magic to ensure its success.'

I exchanged a delighted glance with Raven. 'That's wonderful news!' I said. 'I can't wait to see it happen!' Then, finally, I could let go of the guilt I'd been carrying for breaking the bloody thing in the first place.

After dinner, we followed Abaddon into the large hall where the mirror frame lay on a wooden table. As the previous night, a fire blazed in the hearth. The warlock sorted through a pile of scrolls and lit candles, preparing for his magical endeavour. We stood watching, eager to witness what would happen next. After focusing his energy, he spoke an incantation with a booming voice:

Mirror, mirror, shattered and broken
Reflect no more, magic unspoken
Fear no longer, for I bring a cure
A gem of power, so magically pure

By the power of this glowing stone
I call upon all magic known
And as these incantations pass
They will replace this mirror's glass

By the power of this ancient art
I repair your broken heart
Mirror, mirror, be whole and strong
Reflect once more your magic song!

A strange, prismatic light pulsed through the room, casting dancing rainbows of colour on the wall. The sparkling moissanite gemstone resting on the centre of the mirror blazed and flashed with sparkling intensity. It was breath-taking, and for a moment I almost believed it would never end.

But unexpectedly, the light condensed into one spot—the moissanite gem. Rivers of silver glass poured out from the gemstone in impossible volumes, spreading out in all directions. By the time it filled the entire mirror frame with magical glass, the gem had disappeared. The light faded away.

Raven couldn't contain his excitement any longer. He stepped forward. 'Yes!' he yelled, throwing his arms up in triumph.

Unfortunately, this surge of joy was too much for him, and his curse kicked in yet again. He morphed instantly into a raven in a burst of blinding light. With a flurry of wings, he flapped frantically around us before he ultimately settled on Abaddon's shoulder.

The warlock brushed him off. 'What an irritating curse,' he muttered dryly.

'Oh, Raven!' I said. Now what? Should I wait until he changes back? How long would that take? How would I get him home otherwise? On my shoulder like a pirate's parrot? That would hardly do.

Raven flew up and perched at the top of a bookcase, where he sat and bobbed his feathered head up and down, as if he were silently dancing to some unheard beat.

'Your mirror is ready,' Abaddon said with a tired sigh, swaying in exhaustion. 'That spell took a lot out of me. I must sleep and regain my energy. I assume you'll be leaving in the morning?'

'If Raven transforms back into his human form by then, yes. This mirror is too heavy and bulky for me to carry on my own.'

Abaddon's eyelids were already drooping. 'Take Zara with you. She can help. Your friend can wait here or fly back. Now, if you'll excuse me, I must sleep.'

He trudged out of the room, leaning heavily on his cane. Zara hesitated a moment and then raced to his side, took his arm and helped him towards his bedroom.

I stared up at Raven, whose beady eyes watched me from the top of the bookcase. 'Couldn't you have kept your emotions in check?'

Raven cawed. I assumed that meant 'no'.

I GLANCED OVER AT ZARA, who had returned a moment ago from helping Abaddon. I was about to bid her good night, but stopped short. She appeared pale, and her eyes were wide.

'Zara, what's wrong?' I asked, my heart pounding in my chest.

She hesitated before responding, her voice barely a whisper. 'I can't stay here any longer. Abaddon is so mean to me.' She peered around nervously, as if expecting someone or something else to be lurking in the shadows.

I threw an arm around her shoulders and hugged her tightly. 'It's okay. We'll leave in the morning. You can stay with us in Kingston upon Thames until you decide what you want to do and where you want to go.' The words were out of my mouth before I had time to think it through. Aunt Ruth would no doubt have something to say about this arrangement! But Zara needed my help, and I wasn't about to let her down.

Zara smiled gratefully at me. 'Really? Thank you!'

'Plus,' I added quickly, 'I'll need your help to carry the mirror, anyway. That's your excuse to come with me.'

She looked puzzled. 'Where's Raven?'

I gestured with my head. 'Up there.'

'I see.' She sighed. 'I'll fetch some birdseed later. And there's a birdcage around somewhere. I'll try to find it.'

Raven squawked and flapped his wings angrily.

'It's for the best,' I said, trying to reassure him. 'You can't fly all the way home.'

It seemed like he glared at me in response, but how could you really tell with birds? Their expressions are so hard to interpret sometimes.

I turned back to Zara. 'Do you think Abaddon will come after you?'

Zara frowned. She exhaled slowly. 'Maybe. I won't hang around long at your place in case he does. Maybe only two or three nights until I can find somewhere else and get myself sorted with a job or something. I need to disappear.'

My breath hitched slightly at her words. 'Disappear?'

'Yeah.'

'All right, if that's what you want...'

We hugged each other goodbye for the night and went our separate ways.

What was going on between Abaddon and Zara? My curiosity was eating at me, but I'd probably never discover the truth.

I WAS SO EXHAUSTED from spending half the day walking around Berwick upon Tweed that I practically dragged myself up the stairs and into the bedroom.

But I wasn't yet ready to sleep. No, I wanted to reach out to Rose first. It had only been two evenings ago that I'd spoken to her, but a lot was going on in her life right now. She had her university study, a new relationship and the inconvenience of her useless father staying in her flat—in her room, no less. She was probably feeling overwhelmed and needed someone to talk to.

Sitting back in bed, I opened up the video chat and waited for her to answer. It would be morning in New Zealand. She might have left for university already. I had no way of knowing.

After a few moments, she answered, a wide smile curling across her lips when she saw me. Sunshine cascaded through the kitchen window behind her. Her girlfriend Madison was beside her, mostly out of frame.

'Hi, Mum,' Rose said cheerfully. 'How are you?'

'Exhausted,' I replied with a yawn. 'I forgot to tell you last time I'm on a mini break, sorting out something for Aunt Ruth. I'm staying in a lovely quaint town up near the Scottish border. I did heaps of walking today, and these days, that wears me out more than when I was your age.'

Rose laughed before firing back teasingly, 'Oh, but did you have fun?'

I couldn't go into the details. 'More or less. Is your father still staying with you, being a complete nuisance?'

Rose chuckled. 'No, I made him move out. He set up an office and apparently rented one of those fancy apartments in Oriental Bay.'

'It must have cost him a fortune. I'm glad he's out of your place now. You can have your room back!'

'Well... Madison and I are ready to share a room, actually. I'm moving into hers. We'll sublet my old room.'

'Oh, wow. I'm glad it's going so well for you.' Her relationship was developing fast. I hoped it wouldn't end in tears, with me so far away. I could only provide so much comfort from afar.

'Yeah, it is. We're in love.' Rose beamed.

At that moment, a smashing sound came through the phone.

My heart beat wildly, and my eyes widened. 'What was that noise?' A burglar breaking through a window? A car crash outside their flat?

Rose giggled. 'That's Maddie. She's getting creative.'

Madison's paint-streaked face appeared in the frame for a few moments. 'Hi, Heather,' she said, flashing me a bright smile.

'Hi,' I replied belatedly, but she'd disappeared from view. My racing heart eased back to normal speed.

'I've got more news, Mum,' Rose said.

'You have?' *What now?* I could hardly keep up with my daughter.

'Yeah. Psychology isn't my thing anymore.' Her eyes shone with excitement, and I braced myself for whatever came next.

'So... you're going to switch to another subject next semester?'

'Oh no, Mum. I'm dropping out altogether. I'm planning on making art with Madison.'

Don't panic, I told myself, panicking. 'You're leaving university to smash up teacups and paint them?'

Rose shook her head, grinning mischievously. Beside her, Madison laughed raucously.

'What's so funny?' I asked, irritated. 'You were going to study hard, get a degree and have a career. Are you going to throw that away?'

'No, Mum.' Rose's expression became more serious. 'And it's not about me smashing up teacups. That's Maddie's thing. I'm going to smash up plates and bowls and turn them into modern art pieces.'

I blinked twice, trying to process this information. My daughter was ditching her degree to smash up plates. 'And how do you plan to pay your bills doing that?'

'It's modern art, Mum. I'll sell it. Maddie sold her last work for twelve thousand dollars.'

That left me speechless. Twelve grand was two months' pay for a teacher. I'd obviously worked in the wrong profession. I should have been smashing things up and painting them instead.

'It might sound silly, Mum, but we're serious about this—it's all or nothing with us!' she exclaimed.

There was something endearing about her dedication and passion that made me smile despite myself.

Chapter 25

AFTER OUR CALL, I RUMINATED on what Rose was planning to do. It may not have been what I'd desired my intelligent daughter would do, but it was ultimately her life and her choice. I wouldn't discourage her or hold her back the way my father had done with me at her age. That merely drove me into the clutches of a man like him, and it certainly hadn't turned out well.

I went downstairs to make myself a hot drink and encountered Mrs Brown in the kitchen, elbows deep in the sink. When I asked if I could make a hot chocolate or something, she insisted on doing it for me, despite my protestations that I could do it myself. She sent me packing from the kitchen two minutes later so she could get back to work uninterrupted. I hoped Abaddon was paying her well, because she didn't seem to ever stop for a rest.

I wasn't back in my room for long before Rachel video called me. I was expecting her call and answered immediately. She was calling from her car, using the hands-free link.

'Hey, Rach, how are you feeling? Not still cut up over your break-up?'

'Hey, Heather. No, I'm totally over that. Work has been crazy busy, though. I'm on my way there now. I thought I'd check in with you and see how you're doing.'

'I'm good. We're still away in Berwick upon Tweed, but we're going back to Kingston upon Thames tomorrow.'

'We?' she asked, shooting me a mischievous look.

Oops. 'Raven and I.'

She made an exaggerated expression of surprise, and I hoped she would not drive off the road. 'Ooh! Is your romance on now, girlfriend?'

I sighed. 'No. We needed to do something for Aunt Ruth. It wasn't a romantic trip.' Unluckily for me.

Undeterred by my answer, Rachel winked slyly at me with a glint in her eyes. 'Maybe next time, then. Anyway... what else is going on?'

I played dumb and replied innocently, 'What do you mean?'

'I mean, you've been very secretive about your new life in England.' She paused, and her expression became more serious. 'You always seem on edge and you avoid my questions. I want to understand what's going on and help you however I can, Heather. I know something has unsettled you in a major way. It's not only your aunt's condition, is it?'

This was the moment. She was waiting for my reply with one eyebrow quirked, her lawyer expression in overdrive.

If I continued to lie to Rachel and pretended my life was normal, like I'd been doing up to now, she would know for certain I wasn't ever planning on being honest about what was really going on with me. She'd think I didn't trust her. It could irretrievably damage our friendship.

But if I told her about my weird new life, would she believe me? Or would she think I needed mental health support?

There truly was only one thing I could do. This was Rachel I was talking to. My long-time best friend. I took a deep breath. 'I think you better pull over and park somewhere.'

'Oh, it's that serious? Let me just—'

The blare of a horn came through the phone, and I saw Rachel glance towards the rear-view mirror. 'The fucking asshole behind me was tailgating. That moron was the one thumping the horn.'

I nodded, unsurprised. Christchurch drivers had a poor reputation.

'Okay, I'm parked and settled, waiting for whatever you're going to tell me,' Rachel said. 'You have my full attention.'

'Okay... so... I'm a witch,' I said as matter-of-factly as I could.

Rachel tilted her head and didn't answer for several moments. 'Girlfriend, you're many things, but you don't deserve to call yourself a bitch. That's a bit over the top.'

My shoulders sagged in exasperation. 'Not bitch with a "B". Witch. With a "W".'

Now both of her eyebrows shot up. 'A witch. As in, the "Double, double, toil and trouble; Fire burn and cauldron bubble," type of witch?'

Rachel knew her Macbeth. 'That's the one. "By the pricking of my thumbs, something wicked this way comes," but I'm no wicked witch—just an ordinary midlife woman with some extraordinary abilities. I did basic magic today, actually.' I cringed inside. To my friend, I must sound completely nuts.

Her eyes narrowed sceptically. 'You're saying you can do magic spells? Are you for real? What makes you think you're a witch, Heather?'

'Aunt Ruth is a witch too,' I said, determined to make her believe me. She deserved to know the truth about me and my new life, however hard it might be for her to accept.

'Is that so? Did she tell you that, or is it only your opinion? Do you have any evidence of what she said?' Ever the lawyer, Rachel had to ask for proof before believing anything.

'I've seen her doing magic,' I replied. 'There's no doubt about it. She's been teaching me, and I've been working on a correspondence course on witchy things.'

'Witchy things?' Rachel stared at me incredulously. An expression of utter shock spread across her face. 'You aren't kidding, are you? I'm getting very worried about you, Heather.'

'Don't worry about me. It's all true. This is the secret part of my new life you suspected I was keeping hidden from you.'

Rachel nodded, her gaze never leaving mine. 'Okay, then, if you can do magic, do some right now while I'm watching.'

I'd expected that, but I still wasn't prepared for it. 'There's not much I can do yet,' I said cagily.

'Is that so?' Rachel asked, raising one eyebrow.

I was familiar with her tone. I'd heard it many times when she'd recounted how she had questioned people whom she knew were lying to her.

What could I do? Make it rain in my room? Create a gale that would blow the window out? My skills were limited, and my control was sketchy.

Or was it? I'd watered the peonies back home without drowning them. Okay, the wind chimes disappeared in an uncontrollable gale, but fifty per cent was a pass.

'Watch closely,' I said, and pointed my phone camera towards a vase of fresh flowers sitting on the desk by the window.

'What am I watching for?' came Rachel's voice. I could no longer see her. I made the witchy sign, extended an arm towards the vase and visualised it rising from the desk, lifted and buoyed by gentle air currents I stirred up in the room. It did so, slowly.

'That's an impressive trick,' Rachel said with a mix of bewilderment and admiration. 'How did you do it? This is what you mean, isn't it? Magic tricks, like a stage magician.'

I groaned inwardly. How could I make her believe me? I concentrated harder, focusing all my magical energy, and the flowers rose out of the vase, which remained suspended in mid-air.

'Wow! That is so incredible! Are you doing that with invisible wires, or is it a mirror trick of some kind?'

'Neither,' I snapped, regretting my tone as soon as the words left my lips. In an instant, the vase dropped to the desk with a heavy thud, spilling water across the surface and onto the floor. Above, the flowers hovered in place.

Rachel remained silent.

What else could I do to prove I was casting real magic? Weather spells... then it struck me. I could summon heat, like the heat of a summer's day. An exceptionally hot summer's day.

'Keep watching,' I said, conjuring a new spell in my mind.

The warmth hit me like when I'd stepped off the plane in Singapore, but fiercer. Instantly, sweat seeped from my pores. It ran from my forehead into my eyes, stinging them, but I kept my concentration.

'What's happening?' Rachel asked. 'The flowers are drooping.'

They were more than drooping. They were wilting. Dying. Before my stinging, sweat-filled eyes, and Rachel's, watching with amazement from twenty thousand kilometres away, the hovering flowers withered and shrivelled.

'Do you believe me now?' I asked, turning the phone around so I could see Rachel.

My friend blinked a few times before finding her voice. 'That's unbelievable... I don't know how you did that.'

I exhaled heavily. My friend still had doubts. 'Okay, your turn. Tell me what to do with the dead flowers. Not anything crazy like bringing them back to life or something—that's impossible. Tell me where to put them.'

'Okay... put them back in the vase.'

The vase lay on its side on the desk. This would be a real stretch for me, like threading a needle by blowing on the thread. Did I have this much control over my fledgling magic? There was only one way to find out. I turned the phone around again so Rachel could watch.

Gently, I eased the air currents around the dried-up remains of the withered flowers. They dropped quickly at first, bounced off the desk and fell almost to the floor, miraculously still holding their shape as if they were tied together. A new gust sent them flying up too fast, and they overshot the edge of the desk. I was losing control of them, and I boosted the air currents to force the flower bundle into a loop. I visualised them flying into the vase, and to my relief, they powered in, bumping the vase along the desk.

'That's absolutely amazing, Heather.'

'Thank you.' I turned the phone around and wiped my forehead. I was sweating profusely. I closed my eyes for a moment and concentrated on reversing the summer heat wave I'd created in my room. Also, I got up and opened the window. The cool night air was refreshing.

'It wasn't a complete success, though,' Rachel said. 'You jammed those flowers back into the vase upside down. The stems are poking out of the top.'

I gritted my teeth. 'I told you I'm new to this whole thing, okay?'

'Why are you sweating so much? Are you ill? Do you have a fever?'

'No, it's because I created heat to make the flowers wilt. Like I moved the air to make them and the vase move.'

'With magic,' Rachel said. This time, she didn't sound as sceptical.

'Yes. With magic. As I said before.'

My friend regarded me carefully for what seemed a long time, though it was probably only a few seconds. 'Okay, I believe you,' she finally said. 'I can tell you're not making it up.'

A wave of relief swept through me. 'Thank you, Rach. I'm glad I don't have to conceal this part of my new life from you anymore. Keeping it bottled up was making me anxious.'

'Well, two decades of being in court with some of the most accomplished liars in the country has honed my sense for detecting bullshit.'

'Accomplished liars? You mean criminals?'

'The lawyers, of course.'

'Oh. Right.' I guess that made sense.

'This is going to take me some time to get used to. Magic—real magic.' She shook her head. 'And my best friend is a witch. Is there anything else you want to tell me? Now that I'm already in shock, you may as well hit me with everything. You're not a vampire or something, are you?'

Here we go. 'No, I'm not a vampire. But there is something else. I can see ghosts, too, and I can talk to them. I'm friendly with the ghosts at Chirtlewood, especially the countess. Her name is Charlotte, and she died nearly four hundred years ago. There's also a shy girl called Maisey, who led an extremely sad life.'

Rachel's eyebrows quirked again. 'Ghosts? Ghosts are real too?'

'They sure are. I even saw my mother's ghost back home.'

'Wait, are you saying everyone's a ghost after they die?' Rachel asked, her eyes widening. 'That's even more scary than witchcraft.'

'No, only those people who choose to remain behind for whatever reason become ghosts.'

She shook her head. 'This is getting too much for me. I'm going to have to call in sick to work. I'll need the day to process all this. Maybe the rest of the week. I'll work from home when my mind settles down.'

'There's one more thing.'

'There is?' An edge of desperation and incredulity had crept into Rachel's voice.

'The reason I can't have sex with Raven is because he got cursed by an ex-girlfriend, who—'

'Don't tell me. She was a witch, right?'

'Yep. You got it.'

'So... she cursed her ex so he can't have sex anymore, is that it?'

'No, it's more than that. Whenever he gets too excited or happy, the curse triggers, and he shifts into the form of an actual raven. He doesn't become human again for about a day.'

A long pause followed my statement—unsurprising, since it sounded absolutely wild. Rachel finally broke the silence with a sigh. 'That is some mean scorned bitch.'

I sighed. 'Yeah. Anyway, he and Aunt Ruth are trying to find a way of breaking the curse.'

Again, Rachel was silent for some time. I waited patiently. This was so much for her to take in. At least she seemed to accept that what I had told her was the truth.

'Your aunt's got a large house, hasn't she?' Rachel asked. 'Plenty of room for visitors?'

'Yes, but—' I stopped myself short, realising where Rachel was going with her line of questioning. She had already made up her mind.

'Okay. This is what I'm going to do. I have to finish this important case, which might take a couple of weeks. After that, I'm getting on a plane and coming over to see you. I've got to see all this for myself in person.'

I smiled into the phone, my heart lifting in anticipation. 'That would be wonderful! Oh, I'd love to see you. Of course, you can stay here as long as you want.' I was sure Aunt Ruth wouldn't mind, but I'd ask her in the morning.

'Right. I'm going to buy a strong coffee and take it home. I need time to think all this through. Are you going to be okay, Heather?'

'Yes, I am. Truly. Are you? Drive safely, okay?'

'I will. Let's talk again soon.'

We ended the call. I was still standing by the window, looking out at the night sky. The chill in the air was refreshing on my cooling skin, and I was more comfortable now. My room had cooled down too. I went to the bed and lay down, not even bothering to change into my nightgown.

Despite my exhaustion, I couldn't sleep. Everything kept whirling around in my mind like a hamster on a wheel. Was Rose making a dreadful mistake, or would things work out for her? Did Rachel truly believe me? Would she fly over for a visit like she said she would? Was there something in the spell book to help Aunt Ruth? What would happen to Zara? Would Abaddon come after her and insist she return home with him? Could Lydia and I uncover the secret behind Jane Middlemore's death? Would Raven's curse ever be lifted? Could I ever have a relationship with him without him flying off after a kiss or a flirtatious comment?

Eventually, sleep overtook me, but I tossed and turned until the morning light came streaming in.

Chapter 26

THE EARLY MORNING SUN was peeking over the horizon when I awoke to the sound of Zara packing her things in the adjoining room. I quickly got dressed and went to her room, only to find that she had already filled two large suitcases with her clothes and essential items.

'Woah,' I said, lifting one of the large bags. 'You weren't kidding about leaving.'

'I'm taking all my personal possessions,' she replied.

We went downstairs together, Zara hauling one bag and me carrying the other. I also lugged the birdcage that Zara had found. Wrestling the luggage downstairs did no favours for my dodgy knee, which started twinging immediately.

Raven was waiting for us at the bottom of the stairs, perched on a windowsill, and I enticed him to get inside the cage. He poked his beak in my direction, perhaps in annoyance, then waddled in. I desperately hoped he wouldn't revert to human form while he was inside. The cage's delicate bars would shatter if he did, but it might be painful for him.

Zara and I carefully manoeuvred the magic mirror from its resting place into the hallway, where we leaned it against the banister at the bottom of the stairs.

'Now what?' Zara whispered, observing me with worried eyes.

I guessed what she was thinking. Should we say goodbye to Abaddon or just go? I hadn't seen him yet that morning. My stomach rumbled. Neither had we had breakfast.

A door down the hallway banged open, and Mrs Brown ventured through at a leisurely pace, shaking her head fiercely. 'Yer no thinking of leaving without any breakfast, are ye? I've got hot porridge on the stove fer ye both, with a sprinkling o' brown sugar tae add tae it. Go into the dining room, and I'll bring it tae ye in a minute.' She glared at us as if we were about to commit a heinous crime by skipping breakfast, then turned and headed back towards the kitchen.

As if he had been summoned by the racket, Abaddon stormed downstairs, his face livid with anger and outrage when he noticed Zara with two large packed suitcases. It was obvious she intended to leave for good.

'What is the meaning of this?' he snapped, his deep voice echoing through the house. 'You can't just walk out of here! You have a duty to me!' His anger was so intense it seemed like the walls of the room shook from it. His menace was somewhat undermined by his sea-blue flannel pyjamas adorned with cartoon rockets.

I gulped and tried my best to keep my composure amidst his ire. 'Ah... Zara wanted to get an early start.'

Zara trembled but stood defiantly before Abaddon, her mouth set in a determined line and her grey eyes blazing. 'I'm done being under your thumb! I've had enough of this place, and it's time for me to move on!'

Abaddon's mouth curled in a wicked sneer. 'If you're planning on not coming back, then you're not taking the mirror with you. That will stay here with me.'

I clenched my fists as anger bubbled up within me. I stepped between them, my outstretched hands keeping them apart. 'That's outrageous, Abaddon. I've paid you for fixing the mirror. You can't keep it like a hostage because Zara wants to leave home.' I paused for effect, glaring at him. 'It doesn't belong to you.'

Seeing he was outnumbered, Abaddon crossed his arms tightly across his chest and scowled. 'This is all your fault.' He jabbed an accusing finger at me. 'You've put ideas into her head. She needs to stay with me so I can straighten out her misbehaviour. She can't move out until I say so. And for your part in this, I'm keeping the mirror until she agrees not to leave.'

I scowled back at him.

The dining room hall banged open, and Mrs Brown stuck her head out. 'Porridge is served. Get it while it's hot.'

WHY HAD I BEEN SO FOOLISH as to trust the warlock? Aunt Ruth and Raven had both warned me to watch out for him, but I'd blithely gone ahead with my plan.

He'd betrayed me. It was clear the mirror was an artefact of immense magical power, and he wanted to keep it for himself.

I fumed. I couldn't physically take it away from him, even with Zara's help. He was much stronger than us. Raven was in no condition to help us. And if we did get it away when he was unaware, the weight of everything would mean a slow and clumsy escape. Abaddon would catch us with a few of his long strides.

I thrust these thoughts aside. 'You can't do this!' Fury lent my voice a shrill edge. 'That mirror belongs to my aunt. I paid you to fix it. You can't keep it.'

Confusion flashed across the warlock's face. 'I don't intend to keep it,' he replied evenly, his anger fading as quickly as it had arisen. 'All I want is for Zara not to leave home. She's too young and... and impulsive. You've obviously convinced her to move permanently to Kingston upon Thames with you.'

'I have not! It was Zara who said she wanted to leave home,' I protested quickly.

'Heather!' Zara shouted.

Too late. My big mouth was causing trouble again. What had I done? By blurting out my thoughts without filtering them, I'd made things much worse. Now the warlock would be even more furious.

He wasn't. Abaddon staggered back as if I'd pushed him. Crestfallen, he lowered his head. He muttered a plaintive groan before he raised his head to meet Zara's gaze. His eyes glistened.

'I don't understand,' he said, his voice thick with emotion. 'Why do you want to leave, Zara? After all I've done for you? All I will do for you?'

Oh, I don't know. The beating? The verbal humiliation? The tedious chores Zara said he'd given her?

'I have to get away,' Zara said. 'I can't stay here with you after—' She faltered.

Abaddon's mouth was set in a grim line. 'That's exactly why you have to stay,' he said firmly.

'After... what?' I asked. This piqued my curiosity. What could be so awful that Zara wanted to just up and leave?

'Never mind,' Abaddon said quickly, brushing over the topic of conversation as if it were nothing more than an annoying fly to be swatted away.

We stood in a circle in the hallway, eyeing each other, seemingly at a stalemate. Abaddon's glare could cut glass. Zara scowled, yet seemed edgy. I struggled to stop myself from facepalming at the situation.

In his cage on the floor, Raven squawked loudly, as if he were a tiny prisoner demanding freedom. I glanced at him and shrugged. If he was trying to tell me something, I had no idea what he meant.

'This isn't getting us anywhere,' I said with an exasperated sigh. 'I have to get the magic mirror home to Aunt Ruth so she can use it to try to heal herself. And there's no way I can carry it by myself. I need Zara.'

Abaddon narrowed his eyes and pointed at the cage. 'You could wait until Raven changes back to human form.'

'That could take all day. Then we won't get home until tomorrow night. I don't want to waste time. Why should my aunt have to wait because of your disagreement with your assistant?'

'My assistant?' Abaddon almost choked on the last word. 'Zara is my daughter.'

Chapter 27

MY JAW DROPPED SO LOW I thought it might have detached and rolled along the hall. 'Your daughter?'

'Yes,' Abaddon said. 'Didn't she tell you?'

'No. She said she was your assistant.' I contemplated Zara, expecting an explanation, but she avoided my gaze.

'I've been mentoring her, of course. Our family heritage passes down magical power at puberty. So, in a way, I may have treated her as an assistant or apprentice since she gained her magical abilities.' Calmer now, the warlock turned to Zara and gave her a kind, yet pointed, stare. 'You've made your feelings about the matter clear. Go, then. You can return anytime. Also, I will visit you soon to ensure you are faring well.' He clicked his tongue and turned his attention to me. 'I hate to leave home, but in this case, I insist I visit to check up on Zara.'

Zara muttered something unintelligible. I assumed it was about her wish to disappear. I would not mention that in front of Abaddon, but I'd talk to her about it later.

'I will make sure she's all right,' I promised with a reassuring nod.

'I'll be okay,' Zara snapped, giving me a firm glare. 'Stop fussing, the pair of you. You're like two clucking old hens—'

'We're not old,' we said in unison.

'Whatever. Can we go now? We don't want to miss the train.'

'Yes. Fine. Travel safely.' Abaddon opened the front door and held it.

Zara slung her bags over her shoulders and grabbed one end of the mirror. I took the other and lifted the birdcage with my other hand. 'Don't walk too fast for me,' I said.

'But what about the train?' she replied. 'It's not going to wait for us, is it?'

We stumbled towards the open door, slightly unbalanced by our encumbrances, like little kids in a three-legged race.

'Wait!' Abaddon said.

We stopped. I faced him. *What's the problem now?*

He unclasped something from around his neck. It glittered pink in the morning light. The pendant of forgiveness!

'I think you should have this,' he said to Zara, putting it around her neck and tucking it carefully inside her top. 'It helped me find some forgiveness... Maybe it can help you do that too.'

How mysterious. What does Zara need to be forgiven for? Perhaps he thinks she might feel guilty for leaving him. But why? All kids move out eventually. My daughter did it earlier in the year. It's part of growing up.

'Thanks.' Zara accepted the pendant. 'We'd better be going now. Bye... Dad.'

She trundled off. As I held the other end of the mirror, I had no choice but to tread after her at her pace. I gave a brief smile to Abaddon as I passed him. His icy eyes drilled into me, and he didn't return the courtesy.

Zara and I stumbled along the driveway, carrying the heavy and awkward mirror between us, our strides unsynchronised. We tried to settle into a steady pattern, but it was useless. We had too much to carry, it was all too heavy and we'd drop the mirror if one of us took a wrong step.

'Zara, stop a minute. This isn't going to work. I'll call a taxi.'

We lowered the mirror and leaned it against our legs for support. I put the birdcage next to it and pulled out my phone. A quick search brought up the number for a local taxi firm. I asked them to come quickly.

Less than ten minutes later, we were at the train station. I bought the tickets. The train wouldn't arrive for another ten minutes, so we bought muffins and coffee from the station café to take with us. It was even more of a struggle with everything else we had to carry, but we needed something to eat and drink. By the time we'd finished arguing with Abaddon, we'd run out of time to enjoy Mrs Brown's porridge. She'd probably never forgive us.

And now we had to hurry. The train's engine noise rose above the surrounding conversations in the café.

'It's nearly here,' I said urgently as we emerged onto the platform. The train's vibrations reverberated through the station.

'Don't worry. We'll make it,' Zara said, glancing over her shoulder as she moved.

The train station platform wasn't level. She stumbled over a bump, falling forward and pulling the mirror with her. It jerked out of my grasp. Zara tumbled to the asphalt. Our breakfast hurtled towards the track. The mirror went with it, headed towards certain destruction.

'No!' I screamed. Zara was falling safely onto the platform itself, but the mirror would be smashed to smithereens by the oncoming train.

Time slowed to a fraction of its normal speed. Or maybe my thoughts and reactions had sped up because of surging adrenaline. I hastily made the witch sign on my hand.

I reached out with one arm as if I could grab the mirror, desperately willing to turn back time for even a couple of seconds so I could stop Zara from falling and sending the mirror flying. That was impossible, though.

If only someone or something supernatural could stop the mirror from crashing onto the track in front of the train. If only I could cast a spell to save it...

And then I remembered.

I did have enough power, enough magic within myself. The fingers of my outstretched hand tingled. The air around my hand shimmered with an incandescent glow.

A mighty gust of wind arose from nowhere. It caught the mirror as it dived over the platform edge and lifted it up.

From her prone position on the ground, Zara gasped as the mirror, lifted by the sudden wind, swivelled to an upright orientation and came back at us. She barely had time to duck before the frame flew over her.

It flew at me like a rugby forward. I braced myself with one foot back and caught the edges of the frame as it slowed and halted its flight before me.

The mysterious gust died as quickly as it had appeared. The train pulled in to a stop moments later.

Zara got to her feet and shot me a questioning glance. 'What just happened?'

I was stunned by what I'd achieved. 'That wind... it came from nowhere,' I said cautiously.

'Not nowhere.' Her eyes filled with admiration and awe. 'You cast a spell, didn't you? But how did you summon a powerful gale like that so quickly without an incantation?'

My heart thumped against my ribs as I drew in a deep breath. 'I—I visualised it.'

Zara's eyes widened. 'That's incredible.'

I shifted my grip on the heavy frame. 'Let's get on the train with all our stuff. Can you help me carry this?'

A squawk on my left drew my attention. Raven! I'd dropped the birdcage when I grabbed the mirror, and he was not happy about it.

I bent down. 'Are you okay in there, my avian friend?' I teased.

He flapped his wings, his sharp eyes drilling into mine.

'Is Raven all right?' Zara asked.

'Maybe a little shaken, but otherwise unharmed. Quick, let's get on board before the train leaves without us.'

I lifted the birdcage up onto the train, then stepped up with one end of the mirror. Zara took the main weight of it and pushed it the rest of the way in. She climbed up herself to get inside as the bell rang.

The doors closed. We'd been the last passengers to board.

'Did anyone see what happened out there?' I whispered.

Zara shrugged. 'I don't think so. Where are we going to store the mirror? And the birdcage? And my cases?'

'On the floor between the seats. I see some free seats. There's plenty of room for our things and us.'

The train lurched forward, catching us off balance for a moment, before it smoothly picked up speed.

We sat and arranged our luggage. I kept one hand on the mirror so it wouldn't topple and put Raven's cage between my feet so it wouldn't slide if the train halted.

Then I thought of something. 'Oh! The pendant. Do you still have it? Or is it lying on the platform behind us?'

Zara's hand immediately darted to her neck, and she felt for the gemstone on the chain. 'Yes, it's still there.'

'Good.' My curiosity had picked up. 'Raven and I got it for Abaddon. Why did he give it to you?'

Zara stared out the window as the train left the small town and entered the countryside. She didn't answer me.

Chapter 28

THE TRAIN JOURNEY HOME seemed to take forever, and by the time we arrived back in Kingston upon Thames, it was late in the evening.

I stepped out onto the platform, relieved to be home, carrying the birdcage with Raven inside. Zara followed me, her bags over her shoulders. A helpful passenger assisted us to get the unwieldy mirror off the train.

We caught a taxi to Aunt Ruth's house. It went up the driveway at my request and let us out by the porch. Raven flapped and squawked wildly. I put the cage down and quickly opened it. He hopped out onto the porch.

'Here you go, luv,' the taxi driver said, as he manhandled the mirror out of the trunk and propped it against the side of the house. 'Nice place you got here.'

'Thank you.' I gave him a grateful smile and paid the fare before watching him drive off.

A flash of light came from behind me, and Zara gasped. I turned to see what was happening. Raven stood there in human form, breathing hard.

'I didn't know how much longer I could keep from reverting to myself,' he said.

I couldn't help but smile. 'You managed it, though. Maybe you're gaining more control over your raven transformation.'

He shrugged. 'Maybe.'

'How come you're wearing clothes?' Zara asked. 'I thought you'd be naked when you transformed back.'

'Thankfully, no. The curse allows me that shred of dignity.' He picked up the mirror with ease. 'Let's go inside.'

I opened the door, and Raven edged inside with the mirror, which he leaned against the wall. I followed.

Aunt Ruth was waiting in the entranceway, her eyes aglow with anticipation. 'I heard the taxi. I'm so glad you're home.' She beamed and leaned forward in her wheelchair to pull me into a tight hug.

Behind her, Pearl smiled warmly. 'Ruth, if you don't need me anymore tonight, I'll head off.'

'Yes, yes, go, Pearl,' said Aunt Ruth with a fond smile. 'You've been such a great help. Thank you for staying over these past couple of nights.'

'No problem.' Pearl eased past us to the front door and left.

Zara stepped inside and dumped her bags on the wooden floor with a thunk.

Aunt Ruth's face changed from a warm welcome to one of suspicion as soon as she saw Zara. She crossed her arms and furrowed her brow. 'What is she doing here?' she asked, not bothering to hide the disdain in her voice.

I tried to defuse the situation with a joke. 'You know how clumsy I am,' I said with a weak smile. 'If I'd tried to carry the mirror by myself, I'd have broken it again.' The fact that we had dropped it, and I'd saved it, could wait until later.

My feeble attempt at lightening the atmosphere with humour fell flat.

Raven stepped forward. 'I can get some dinner for us, and later you can tell me where you want me to put the mirror. Ruth, have you eaten?'

'I have, thanks, Raven. You go ahead. I'll fetch the spell book and browse through it. I hadn't wanted to do that while Pearl was here. She's not a witch.'

Raven headed towards the kitchen with purposeful strides. He was a superb cook and seemed able to do anything. Whatever he made would be vastly better than the dry sandwiches we'd had on the train and the birdseed he'd nibbled on in the cage.

'Can I stay for a few days?' Zara asked tentatively, her voice trembling with emotion. 'Please?'

'I suppose you can, now that you're here,' Aunt Ruth said flatly. 'You already know where the guest room is.'

I cut in hastily, trying to make excuses for Zara. 'She had to get away from the warlock. You saw how he treated her.'

'Did she need to come here?' Aunt Ruth muttered.

'I've got nowhere else to go,' Zara said. 'I won't be sassy or rude this time, I promise, and it won't be for long. Only until I can sort something out.'

Aunt Ruth's face softened slightly.

'I really needed the help to carry the mirror too,' I said.

Aunt Ruth shifted her attention to me. 'What about Raven? Why didn't he help you?'

I groaned. 'He was so excited when Abaddon fixed the mirror, his curse kicked in. I had to bring him home in a birdcage. It's outside on the porch.'

Aunt Ruth's mouth slowly turned up in a smile. 'How inconvenient,' she said dryly, a twinkle of amusement in her eyes. 'At least he didn't have to fly home.'

LATER THAT EVENING, I texted Lydia to find out if she had made any progress on our investigation.

> Me: *Back in Kingston. Coming back to CH tomorrow :-)*
> Lydia: *Great! Been run off our feet with you away.*
> Me: *Any updates on Jane? Any more clues?*
> Lydia: *I spoke to more locals. Got nothing.*
> Me: *Ok. C U tomorrow.*
> Lydia: *Your turn to get the pastries :-) yum yum*

I was tired from the journey, so I went upstairs to bed early. Aunt Ruth remained in the dining room, browsing through the spell book for healing spells she might try on herself. Raven was bent over his desk, studying intently. Zara had gone to her room with a borrowed mystery novel tucked under her arm.

Chapter 29

THE NEXT MORNING, ZARA was the only one up when I emerged from my room and trudged to the kitchen in search of strong coffee.

'Hi, Heather.' She glanced up at me before returning her attention to the newspaper on the table in front of her.

I made a drink for us both and sat beside her, breathing in the coffee aroma. She had a pen in one hand and circled something in the classifieds.

'You're going through the job ads,' I said.

'Yeah, I'd better find work as quickly as possible. Then I'll look for a flat. I don't want to outstay my welcome here.'

'What kind of job do you want?'

'Waiting tables, retail... anything that'll pay rent and buy food.'

Would Zara fit in at Chirtlewood House? If she kept her sassy attitude in check, maybe... My mind whirred with possibilities.

'I was in the same position as you a few weeks ago, so I understand what it's like. I might know of something for you. I'll check it out today.'

She grinned at me as she sipped her coffee. 'Hey, thanks.'

'No problem.' I swigged some of my coffee and got up to make myself a couple of pieces of wholemeal toast.

Forty minutes later, I arrived at Chirtlewood with a paper bag of Danish pastries and the biggest smile on my face. It had only been a few days, but I'd missed the place. And Lydia, Penny and the mischievous manor house ghosts.

Lydia, Penny and I shared the pastries as usual.

'Any luck finding another person to hire?' I asked.

Lydia shook her head while waving her hand to indicate her mouth was too full to speak. After a while, she said, 'Not yet. The position's advertised at the job centre, but they haven't recommended anyone.'

'We probably won't get anyone,' Penny said dourly.

'Wait a moment,' I said. 'You got me, and I came through the job centre.'

'But you're from New Zealand, not local. Everyone around here knows about the mysterious ghostly behaviour at Chirtlewood, and it puts them off working here.'

'Well, I'm still here. And I know of someone who might be suitable. She's young, sure, but she's smart, and rumours of ghosts won't put her off.' I chose my words carefully. Penny wasn't a witch. I don't think she'd ever had any contact with the Chirtlewood ghosts, unlike Lydia, who knew them well.

'How much younger?' Penny asked.

'She's a teenager.'

Penny's mouth turned down. She didn't seem pleased with the idea.

'It's so hard to get anyone. I'm willing to give her a try,' Lydia said. 'We really do need four people. We all know how hard it is with only the three of us. It was a nightmare with only you and me, Penny.'

'You can say that again,' Penny muttered dryly.

'I'll bring her in a day or two, if it's all right? I can vouch for her—she won't let us down!'

THE MORNING AT CHIRTLEWOOD was busy. More and more tourists turned up to visit the historic manor house. Being summer now, the tourist season was moving into a higher gear.

At lunch, because the weather was nice, I went outside to have my sandwich and fruit in the gardens. We were permitted half an hour. I had a book with me, but today I found it more pleasant to simply enjoy the fresh air and watch the river while I ate.

After a short while, Maisey strolled up to me. I was so pleased to see her, I would have given her a giant hug, but that was impossible. My arms would merely pass through her.

Maisey was a girl of about twelve who'd perished from measles in one of the serfs' cottages. She'd forgotten the years of her birth and death, but it was after the earl and countess had died, because they'd welcomed her ghost into the house after she'd succumbed to the illness.

''Tis grand to hast thee back, Heather,' she said, bouncing from one foot to the other. 'Be thee taking us exploring again anon? 'Tis such merrymaking.'

I laughed fondly at her enthusiasm. 'Not at the moment. I think we're stuck on what to try or who to ask next. We need a new lead.'

Maisey frowned. 'A lead? What might that be?'

'A starting point for a new direction. A clue.'

'Like what sort of thing?' She scratched at her measles spots. Did they itch, even though she'd died two or three hundred years ago?

'I don't know yet for sure, but I have some other news. We might have a new person starting work in the house. Another witch. She's young, only a few years older than you, Maisey.'

'That's nay young,' the girl said. 'That's eld.'

'Well, it's young to me, anyway.'

'A witch? Oh, praise the heavens! That means the lady can see us. We'll hast another living soul to chatter with and befuddle with endless tales of the good eld centuries.'

'She's had a hard time recently,' I said. 'I believe she was treated cruelly.'

'Aye, I too oft did get thwacked even when I wast but a wee thing,' Maisey said sadly. 'That be what happens when ye be bawbling, ain't it? Ye just receive thumps from the big folks.'

'I'm so sorry to hear that,' I said. 'It's not okay for someone to hit others.'

''Twast customary in those fusty days.'

'Anyway,' I said, 'her name is Zara, and it would be great if you introduced yourself to her.'

'Aye.' Maisey smiled brightly. 'I shalt.'

She strolled on with a new bounce in her step.

I gathered my things and sauntered back to the house. My break still allowed me a few minutes, so I fished out my phone and called Inspector Pentecost.

Her voice came through after three rings. 'Pentecost here.' It was sharp and professional, but there was an underlying warmth in her tone that I hadn't noticed before.

'Hello, Inspector. This is Heather Nicholls.'

'I know. Your number is programmed into my phone. Are you calling to ask about the Jane Middlemore case?'

'It's a case now? You're treating it as murder, then?' My throat tightened at the thought of poor Jane.

She paused for a beat before responding. 'I'm regarding it as suspicious, yes.'

I reached the building and paused. 'Are there any new leads?' Might as well get the most out of this conversation while I could.

'You know I shouldn't talk to you about an ongoing investigation.'

'Yes... but Lydia and I have given you some useful information about it.'

The inspector lowered her voice so much I strained to make out her words through the phone. 'I realise that, and for that reason only, I'll let you know we have another eyewitness. A local man jogging with his dog said he saw a woman of Ms Middlemore's description accompanied by another person. They were talking animatedly and walking alongside each other.'

Talking animatedly? Were they arguing or laughing? 'Did he give you a description of the other person?'

'No, he was behind them, but he recognised Ms Middlemore when she turned around once after his dog yapped. Unfortunately, that's all we have for now. We're still no closer to discovering who the mystery individual is.'

I ARRIVED HOME LATER that afternoon, still dwelling on how to make progress on determining the circumstances of Jane Middlemore's death. Was it an accident, suicide or murder?

I entered the kitchen and found Aunt Ruth sitting at the table, her expression utterly miserable, while Raven paced back and forth with a resolute scowl etched across his face.

'What's wrong?' I asked, stopping short. Aunt Ruth's eyes were red, as if she'd been crying. I bent over her and put my arm around her shoulders reassuringly. 'Aunt Ruth?'

She peered at me with glistening eyes. 'I'm all right. It's the disappointment, that's all. I was overcome for a moment.'

'Disappointment?' I turned to face Raven.

His face was a picture of barely concealed fury.

'The warlock tricked us,' he said. 'The mirror doesn't work. Your aunt says Abaddon has magically locked it, and only he has the spell key.'

'That bastard,' I snapped, my hands balling into fists.

Raven crossed his arms, nostrils flaring with indignation. 'If he was here now, I'd—'

'Don't get too excited. Your curse will trigger.'

'Damn it, you're right.' He exhaled loudly, trying to calm himself. 'Let's get ourselves some tea or something and figure out what to do about this mess.'

'Did you call Abaddon?' I asked, anger at the warlock seeping through my veins like liquid fire.

Raven nodded curtly, then let out a sigh of frustration. 'I did, but he's not answering his phone. We should never have trusted him.'

'He'll demand something else,' Aunt Ruth said. 'Copying the spell book and gathering those flowers at midnight wasn't enough, apparently.'

I ran my fingers through my hair. 'We gave him something else,' I said. 'He asked for a potion of forgiveness. We gave him a pendant. He told us it worked.'

'Yet he still locked the mirror,' Aunt Ruth said. 'It's useless to me until he unlocks it.'

Raven brought over a tray of tea and cookies and set it down on the table amidst our conversation. He had calmed down and took a seat next to Aunt Ruth. I sat on the other side of her.

'Does Zara know anything about this?' I asked.

Raven shook his head. 'I asked her. She seemed genuinely surprised at what Abaddon did.'

'Where is she, anyway?'

'Out in the garden,' Aunt Ruth said. 'Just sitting. I don't know what's going on with that girl, but at least she's quiet and not rude for once.'

'She isn't too bad, considering she's a teenager, you know,' I said with a wry smile. I grimaced inside. Rose had been pretty bad at that age, and so had I.

I took a sip of the tea Raven had made. I'd wanted white hot chocolate, but I would not be rude and refuse the drink he'd prepared.

'If we can't contact Abaddon, we might have to go back.' I groaned. That meant at least two more days away from home, the expense of more train fares, and the difficulty of lugging the mirror with us.

'Let's not take the mirror again. I could go up there on my own and confront him,' Raven said, 'and not leave until he agrees to return with me.'

An idea hit me. 'Can't another powerful witch undo Abaddon's spell and unlock the mirror?'

Aunt Ruth shook her head sadly. 'Not without breaking it. Permanently.'

I clenched my fists in frustration. Fuck! I'd put a lot of trust in that damned warlock. I'd done everything he'd asked. Was it all for nothing?

'So... he tricked us, do you think?' I asked Raven, who was chewing his lip, deep in thought.

Raven met my gaze. 'Maybe I was too hasty in saying that. There could be a logical explanation. Perhaps the lock protected the mirror on the journey home, and he'll unlock it as soon as we make contact.'

Aunt Ruth shook her head. 'He'll need to be here to do that.'

Raven set his jaw and straightened up, lifting his chin in determination. 'In that case, I'll set off tomorrow and fetch him.'

'I'll go with you,' I said. That would mean even more days away from Chirtlewood.

With the plan decided, we sat quietly as we finished our drinks. Light rain pattered against the windowpane.

My head buzzed with all the stress of the situation. I'd failed Aunt Ruth. I'd trusted the warlock, and he hadn't kept his side of the bargain. We were back to square one. Worse than that, because several days had passed. Aunt Ruth's September the third date—the day she'd told me would be the date of her death—was steadily creeping closer.

We had to get the mirror unlocked. For Aunt Ruth's sake.

At that moment, an urgent knocking startled us. I glanced at my aunt.

'I'm not expecting anyone,' she said, frowning.

'I'll see who it is.' I stood and strode to the front door. If it was a salesperson, I'd send them packing with a few choice words. My patience was sorely stretched now.

I flung the door open, only to take a step back in surprise.

Abaddon stood there, unsmiling. Water dripped from his cloak. He must have walked from the train station. In one hand, he held a small travelling bag, and in the other, his walking cane, which he leaned on.

His eyes narrowed, and he jabbed the cane toward me with such ferocity it made me recoil slightly. 'I am furious,' he spat out coldly between gritted teeth. 'You and your friend tricked me.'

Chapter 30

HANDS ON HIPS, I GLARED at the warlock in a state of indignation.

'What do you mean? We gave you what you wanted. You double-crossed us. The mirror is magically locked. My aunt can't use it.'

Abaddon entered without waiting for an invitation and threw his soggy cloak onto the coat rack. Water dripped from it onto the wooden floor.

'That was merely a precaution I took to ensure that the forgiveness pendant you gave me actually worked properly.' His expression darkened. 'However, although it seemed to work at first, ultimately, it was a dud.'

'What's going on?' Raven said, coming into the hall. 'Abaddon? Are you here for Zara?'

The warlock turned to Raven. 'No. I came to complain about the pendant.'

My jaw dropped, and I turned to Raven desperately for an idea of what to say. He appeared as clueless as me, so I hastily said, 'But you gave it to Zara.'

'It appeared to have worked its magic on me. I thought I didn't need it any longer. That's why I gave it to Zara. But its power didn't last.'

'Surely, it would only work if you wore it yourself.'

'I think you know why I'm here. I need a new one—a better one. Higher quality, so the forgiveness magic doesn't fade so quickly.'

'Not again,' Raven muttered. 'Is there going to be no end to his ridiculous demands?'

'I heard that. Know this: Until you completely fulfil your side of the bargain, I won't fulfil mine.'

Aunt Ruth rolled into the hallway and glared up at Abaddon from her wheelchair. 'You've got a nerve coming here. Unlock my mirror right away! You can't leave until you've done it.'

Abaddon smiled. 'I've no intention of leaving until everyone is happy.'

Aunt Ruth frowned. Clearly, that wasn't the answer she expected.

'Please explain,' I said, arching my brow. 'Two days ago, you told me how much better the pendant made you feel. Now you're saying its power didn't last?'

'Once you'd all gone, and I was on my own again, the dark thoughts returned. I—' A pained expression filled his face, and he choked on his words. He suddenly seemed vulnerable.

We waited in silence for him to continue, unsure what to say or do.

'I can't get it out of my mind,' he said feebly, no longer the imposing character he usually appeared to be.

'You can't forgive yourself?' I asked cautiously, trying to get some clarity.

His eyebrows flew up at this suggestion. 'What? No, it's not that. I don't need to forgive myself. It's...' He fell silent again.

'Someone else?' Aunt Ruth asked.

Who? Someone close to him? A former lover? Maybe he couldn't forgive Zara for leaving him. Maybe it was someone we hadn't even heard about yet. A million possibilities raced through my mind. Whoever it was, they had hurt him deeply, but I didn't expect Abaddon to tell us the details.

I steeled myself to offer some comforting advice, even though it was well out of my field of expertise. 'If the pendant didn't work for you,' I said gently, 'I don't think a new one will work either. You need to find forgiveness within yourself—in your heart.'

The warlock regarded me with a tortured expression. 'I can't,' he replied hollowly. 'It's beyond me. Honestly, I don't know if I can forgive and forget.'

'All right,' Raven declared. 'I have an idea. We can't help you find forgiveness, but I can help you forget.'

Hope glimmered in Abaddon's eyes. 'You think so?'

'Yes. Come with me into the living room.'

We followed Raven into the living room, where he motioned for Abaddon to take a seat in a comfortable armchair. He did so apprehensively, as if expecting a trick of some kind.

Raven sat opposite him and knitted his fingers together. 'I'm going to hypnotise you,' he said.

Wait, what? Raven can hypnotise people?

'Hypnotise me?' Abaddon replied with a note of disbelief in his voice.

'Yes. It's perfectly safe. All you have to do is relax, listen to my voice and let your worries drift away with each breath you take. I want you to focus on a spot on the ceiling. Any spot will do. Have you done that?'

Abaddon nodded slowly with his lips pursed in concentration as he kept his gaze firmly fixed on what was likely a patch of damp or a crack in the ceiling plaster.

'Keep your eyes on it.' Raven spoke quietly but firmly. 'I am going to count down from ten to one. With each number I say, you will become more and more relaxed until finally you are so tired you will want to close your eyes, and it's perfectly fine to close them. Now I am going to start counting.'

Raven counted slowly, leaving several seconds between each number, but filling the intervals with encouragement for Abaddon to relax and go deeper. Abaddon followed Raven's instructions and slowly relaxed into the chair until his body was limp and his eyes were closed.

'Now, imagine a sandy beach,' Raven said in a soothing, entrancing voice. 'A beach where all your worries can drift away on the tide. In your mind, walk along that beach and feel the warm grains of sand between your toes. There is only peace and tranquillity here. Cast your unwanted thoughts into the sea. Listen to the tide carry them away.'

Abaddon's breathing became deep and steady, like a serene ocean. As Raven spoke, something within my inner core shifted, as if I were in another realm—one of peace and calm.

Time stood still as Aunt Ruth and I watched in awe at the power of Raven's voice over Abaddon's mind and body. It was almost magical how quickly Abaddon had gone from an agitated state of angry confusion to a deep, trance-like state under Raven's influence.

Raven continued. 'You will forget whatever has caused you this distress,' he said calmly. 'When you open your eyes again, it will be as if you are unaware of it. If you become aware of it again, it will be simply a thought with no emotion attached, something about which you feel calm and detached.'

Abaddon appeared entirely captivated by Raven's voice as he continued emphasising his message. Even when I coughed unintentionally, the warlock remained in an altered state of consciousness.

'Abaddon, soon I will count from one to five. With each number, you will allow yourself to move closer to your normal waking state. When I reach the number five, you will open your eyes, and you will feel relaxed and more refreshed than you have been for a long time. You will have a new sense of calm and serenity about you. Now I will start to count.'

Raven counted. I held my breath. How would the warlock emerge from his trance?

When Abaddon opened his eyes, he appeared content and relaxed, as if he'd been sunning himself in the Caribbean for two weeks. He gazed at Raven with awe and respect.

'Do you remember what caused your distress?' I asked, unable to keep my mouth shut.

Abaddon swivelled his head to face me, and he smiled warmly. 'I'm not upset about anything. I feel absolutely wonderful.' His voice was eerily calm.

Raven smiled, then shot me a glance that I think meant 'shut up' before turning back to Abaddon and asking, 'Would you like something to eat and drink? A sandwich and a cup of tea, perhaps?'

'I would absolutely appreciate that,' the warlock replied, 'but first, shall I unlock Ruth's magic mirror?'

Chapter 31

WHILE RAVEN AND AUNT Ruth went with the warlock to watch him remove the magical lock from the mirror, I went outside in search of Zara.

It was late twilight now, but it wasn't chilly at all. The light rain had stopped.

Zara sat in her usual spot under the weeping willow, apparently contemplating everything and nothing.

'Are you okay, Zara?' I asked as I took a seat next to her. 'By the way, Abaddon's here.'

Startled, she swung around, but kept her gaze focused on the ground. 'Oh, Heather, it's you. You surprised me. Yes, I'm fine.'

'You don't seem fine to me,' I prodded.

'I'm not thrilled about the warlock—Dad—turning up unannounced,' she said grimly. 'I wasn't expecting that.'

'No one did.' That's what turning up unannounced generally involves.

She met my gaze at last. 'I don't want to see him.'

'Well, that's your choice, but you might find he's a changed man.' For now.

'Really? How?' Zara asked.

I smiled. 'Raven put him in a trance, and now he's as relaxed as a cat napping on a windowsill. He's forgotten whatever was upsetting him.'

Zara's eyes widened, and her eyes lit up. 'That's... a surprise. I didn't think that was possible.'

'It seems that Raven can help people to see things differently.' And was full of surprises. I had no idea he could do what he'd just done with Abaddon.

Zara stood up. 'Okay, maybe I'll come inside, then.'

We went in. Zara headed to her room, apparently still avoiding Abaddon, and I went in search of everyone else.

Though I had been outside for only a few minutes, the warlock had already unlocked the mirror. Aunt Ruth and Raven were beaming with joy.

I found Abaddon reclining in an armchair in the living room.

'It's all done? So quickly?'

'It is,' the warlock said, 'and what a powerful conduit of magical energy it is. The mirror requires one day to fully recharge its power. By this time tomorrow, your aunt will once again be able to cast her most potent spells.'

A tremendous rush of relief swept through me. 'That's such wonderful news. Thank you so much!'

He smiled kindly. 'You're welcome. One more thing... I know of a recipe for a potion that may help your aunt. No guarantees, though. The recipe is listed in the spell book you allowed me to copy.'

'But you knew it already?'

'I was aware of it, but I did not have all the details committed to memory. Remember, I have a rather extensive collection of magic books in my house.'

The two separate libraries teaming with leather-bound books in Abaddon's mansion sprang to mind. 'I could lose myself in your libraries. Tell me more about this recipe. I guess it must have a set of ingredients?'

He nodded sagely. 'Yes, but most of them are commonplace. Your pantry will have many of them, and the others are all generally available at stores—except for one, which is difficult to obtain.'

Shit. 'How difficult? What is it?'

Abaddon glanced at me with a hint of amusement in his glinting eyes. 'It is a powder made from crushing the petals of green-winged orchids, which must be picked only at midnight.'

'Green-winged orchids?' I gasped. 'But those are the flowers you sent Zara and me to gather for you! Why didn't you tell us what they could be used for at the time?'

'I didn't know if you would fulfil all aspects of your side of our bargain,' Abaddon said carefully. 'But now you have, and I'm happy to share that knowledge with you.'

Great. So, tonight, I'd have to go back and collect more orchids, then figure out how to crush the petals and make the powder. Would it be tricky? Maybe the recipe gives explicit instructions. If not, I might ruin it. I'd never been any good at gardening or baking.

And would those pesky druids be there, ready to pounce on any intruders in their precious orchid field?

Abaddon seemed bemused by my predicament. 'Don't trouble yourself over it.' He reached into a pocket of his robe and withdrew a small vial containing a green powder. 'I have already prepared this vial from the orchids you and Zara gathered.'

Relief flooded through me, but I tamped it down immediately. This wouldn't be freely given. 'What's it going to cost me?' I asked, suspicion shading my voice.

The warlock was taken aback by my question. 'Nothing at all. It's yours. Take it. The only reason I sent you and Zara to collect it was so I could prepare it for your aunt in advance.'

I stared at him with a newfound gratitude. 'Thank you, Abaddon. This is extremely kind of you.' I reached for the vial. Once it was in my hand, I held it aloft, peering at the grainy green particles inside, before I tucked it safely into a pocket, afraid I might drop it.

'Tomorrow, you can purchase any ingredients you don't already have, and your aunt can make the potion and cast the spell.' The warlock smiled gently. 'I hope it works for her.'

I was so overcome with appreciation I almost rushed forward to hug him, but he didn't appear to be the huggy-feely type, so I stayed put and simply said, 'You've been so helpful to us.'

He gave a modest shrug. 'You've helped me, too.'

I sat on the sofa opposite. Abaddon's eyelids gently drooped.

'Are you going home tomorrow?' I asked after a few moments of sitting in silence. 'It would be awesome if you could stay another night. In case we have any trouble with the healing spell.'

'I will stay another night, thank you. I'll be busy during the day, though. I have a funeral to attend.'

'A funeral?' My brow furrowed. 'An acquaintance or—'

His face was sombre. 'My ex-wife.'

His words hit me like a pile of bricks, and a rush of guilt swept through me. Raven and I had put Abaddon under so much pressure when his ex-wife had just died and he might have been grieving.

But he'd never said anything about it. We couldn't have known.

'Were you still close?' I whispered, my heart as heavy as an anchor for him.

He shook his head. 'No, our relationship fell apart years ago, and we barely kept in touch. However, I feel it's my duty to pay my respects.'

'Of course. I understand.' My mind was still reeling from what he must have been going through.

Abaddon opened his eyes fully and gazed at me mournfully. 'She was a witch too,' he mumbled, almost as though he were speaking only to himself. 'I've already mentioned her to you. Her name was Jane Middlemore.'

Chapter 32

I WAS THUNDERSTRUCK. 'Jane Middlemore was your wife?'

Abaddon grimaced, shaking his head. 'My ex-wife.'

'So that means Zara is—'

'Our daughter. Yes.' His jaw tightened slightly. 'Jane is—was—her mother.'

'But she told me the witch's council had taken her away from her mother because her mother was unfit, and they sent her to you so you could teach her witchcraft.'

The corners of Abaddon's lips turned down in a pained expression. 'That isn't entirely true. Once I realised Jane was struggling with her... issues, and it wasn't suitable for Zara to remain there any longer, I took her to my house.' He sighed heavily. 'I've been teaching her everything I know about witchcraft, but she still has much to learn.'

As do I. 'I see. Have you talked to the police about her death?'

His brow furrowed. 'No. I understand she fell in the river when out walking and drowned. Why would I need to talk to the police about that?'

'Never mind. Forget what I said.'

He hesitated. 'I'll show you a photo of our family.' He pulled his wallet from a pocket of his robe, opened it and withdrew a small photograph. He handed it to me with tenderness. 'Here. Have a look.'

I reached for it and stared. It had been taken outdoors somewhere—likely near Abaddon's home—depicting a lush landscape with a lake glistening in the sunlight in the background. Abaddon and a young Zara stood on the left and in the centre, and Jane stood on the right.

'Beautiful,' I said, handing it back.

'Beautiful things seldom last.' He tucked the photo away.

'They can in a photograph,' I said.

The warlock wasn't listening. He unsuccessfully tried to stifle a yawn. 'I must go to bed. My journey today has exhausted me. As I've told you, I rarely travel because I detest leaving home so much. I'm not used to it.'

'Good night, then. And thank you again.'

Abaddon stood, smiled wearily and left the room.

My mind thronging with questions, I went upstairs to my own room and lay on the bed. I needed to get my head around all this. Get it straightened out in my mind, if I could.

So... Abaddon, Zara and Jane were a family. They'd broken up a long time ago. Zara had gone to live with her father three years ago, presumably when Jane's behaviour became too erratic.

But why had Zara lied about it? She'd said the witch's council had uplifted her from her family home.

I pondered this for a minute or two. I should have brought wine upstairs for this. Fortunately, I did have chocolate in the top drawer for these kinds of occasions. A family-sized bar, unopened. That would have to do. I tore open the golden foil wrapping with a satisfying rip and broke off a line of sweet squares, then bit off the first two.

The rich, creamy chocolate melted in my mouth, its sweetness a pleasant distraction for a few moments.

Perhaps Zara had been ashamed of her mother and didn't want to talk about her with me. After all, we'd barely met. It was the simplest explanation, and surely the most likely.

Yet she hadn't mentioned Abaddon was her father, either.

I ate the rest of the row of chocolate and broke off another. One problem with chocolate bar wrappers was the impossibility of wrapping up part of an opened bar. Or so I told myself.

There was no need for Zara to mention Abaddon was her father. But there was no need for her not to mention it either.

I kept eating, savouring the sweet, creamy taste.

That photograph. Inspector Pentecost had found a partial photograph, hadn't she? Obviously, not that one, because the one Abaddon had shown her was complete. But it is easy enough to print another, isn't it? Or a warlock skilled in the discipline of transmogrification, like Abaddon, could magically replace a torn print with ease.

Was Abaddon capable of murder? Is it possible that he travelled to Kingston and killed his ex-wife? Is that why he sent Zara here in his place instead of coming himself to repair the mirror? Because he wanted to—

I shuddered at the macabre thought. It was possible. Anything was possible. But was it likely? What motive did he have?

When did he learn of Jane's death?

I hadn't asked him.

Another line of chocolate disappeared. It was all too easy to eat, the sugar fuelling my brain. Damn it, why did chocolate taste so good? I should control my sweet tooth. Diabetes was a genuine threat.

I couldn't help myself and broke off the next line. Perhaps I wouldn't buy any more chocolate for a few weeks. Days, I mean.

What of the footprint at the riverbank? Inspector Pentecost's forensic people took photos and a cast. They said the print was of a boot.

Was Abaddon wearing boots? Not today, he wasn't, but that meant nothing.

What of the warlock hitting Zara with his walking cane? Why had he done that? He's never admitted doing it. But Zara wouldn't have used magic to hit herself, would she? That was a ridiculous idea.

Was Zara in danger—real danger? If Abaddon had killed Jane, was Zara going to be next?

No. I shook my head. Surely not, especially after Raven's hypnotherapy session with him. Abaddon was much calmer and seemed to have forgotten whatever had caused him distress.

Yet Zara was still afraid of him. She didn't even want to meet his gaze.

When I asked Abaddon if he'd forgiven himself, he'd said he didn't need to forgive himself for anything.

I sighed. It wasn't making sense. Not all of it. But I must be close to working it out.

I glanced at the chocolate wrapper. Its delicious contents were gone. When did I eat it? Oh, shit! I hadn't even noticed! That's what happened when I got deep in thought. No wonder my trousers were getting tight lately.

Tomorrow, I would call Inspector Pentecost. It was time we compared ideas about this case. If we, together with Lydia, put everything together, maybe something would stand out and we could solve this mystery once and for all.

Chapter 33

NEXT MORNING, I GOT up early, before the rest of the house awoke. As much as I loved spending time with Aunt Ruth and Raven, sometimes I craved time on my own to think. Having a coffee and toast usually helped.

The house was quiet for a few minutes, but presently Zara appeared, her hair still tousled from sleep, breaking my solitude.

'I heard you get up,' she said, rubbing her eyes. 'Can I come with you to Chirtlewood to ask about the job?'

With all that had happened with the mirror the previous night, I'd forgotten I'd offered to take Zara with me to work.

'Of course.' I smiled, trying not to show how taken aback I was by her enthusiasm. 'And I'll buy extra pastries today.'

'You have pastries at work?'

I gave a rueful smile. 'Every day. Fortunately, we're all on our feet all day, and up and down the stairs, so we can easily burn off those calories—most of them, anyway.'

'All right. When shall we go?'

'Why don't you get yourself some quick breakfast and then we'll be off? That way, I can show you around before everyone else arrives.'

'Cool. Thanks, Heather.'

She made toast and coffee and sat at the table, fiddling with her phone. I watched her thoughtfully. Jane Middlemore's funeral was today, and she had made no mention of going to it either on her own or with Abaddon. Indeed, if she came with me to Chirtlewood, she would miss it.

Clearly, she hadn't got on with her mother.

I jolted at a sudden thought, almost spilling my drink and causing Zara to glance up. Perhaps she assumed I'd nodded off and woken abruptly, for she quickly returned her attention to her phone.

Did Zara know her mother was dead?

Maybe she didn't. If Abaddon hadn't told her, who else might have? No one. She could be blissfully unaware of what happened to Jane Middlemore. She would have no idea her mother's funeral was today.

Surely, the warlock would have told her. He'd found out somehow. Perhaps by reading the obituaries or a news article on the mysterious death. Or maybe the police had contacted him.

This was a mini mystery in itself.

Should I bring up the subject? I wracked my brain. If Zara already knew about her mother's funeral, she didn't want to talk about it. But if she didn't, it wasn't my place to tell her, was it? Her father should do that.

Zara downed the last of her drink and stood. 'Let's go. I'm keen to see this place after what you've told me about it.'

I stood and followed her into the hallway. Rain pattered on the roof tiles and the tree leaves outside, so I grabbed my coat.

Zara slipped her feet into a pair of sturdy boots. They clonked on the floorboards as she moved, and I worried the noise might wake Aunt Ruth.

She'd worn them before. The night she arrived to help us with the magic mirror and copy the spell book, and she couldn't do either of those things.

That was the evening Jane Middlemore had died.

A chill ran through me. Surely, it was a coincidence?

It had been raining that day, too, and her boots had been muddy. I remembered cleaning up the entranceway later in the evening.

A chasm opened within me. Was all this merely an eerie quirk of timing?

Zara opened the front door and turned expectantly. 'Aren't you coming?'

'Yes. I had my mind on something else.' An idea that kept pounding away in my brain like a battery-operated drummer toy.

I drove us to Chirtlewood. Zara tried to start a conversation a couple of times, but I was too distracted by my own thoughts to listen to her. She gave up. Our journey was only about ten minutes, anyway, so the silence was brief, broken only by our brief stop at the bakery to buy pastries.

The old Triumph crunched over the gravel car park. I stopped, and we entered the house through the back door.

'Oh, wonderful!' Zara gasped, her eyes widening. 'You have a ghost!'

As a witch herself, she could see the young girl peering down from the landing on the stairs.

'More than one,' I said, waving at Maisey.

Zara rushed towards her, but the young ghost vanished. Zara turned back, disappointed.

'She's shy,' I said. 'But once she gets to know you, she's actually really friendly.' *If she gets to know you. If you're working here.*

'Cool. Can you show me around?'

'Sure. Come with me.'

I took Zara on a tour of the ground floor of the manor. We had at least half an hour before Lydia and Penny would arrive, so I took a little time in each room to point out everything worth seeing. 'If you work here, you'll get to shadow each of us in turn so you can pick up lots of information before you're let loose on your own with the tourists.'

Zara nodded, captivated by the seventeenth-century kitchen and its enormous hearth with cooking pots and roasting spits. 'This is amazing.'

'Come upstairs. I'll show you the library and the bedchambers.'

We ascended the staircase, and, before Zara could even ask about them, I drew her attention to the beautifully carved banister rails that were hand-carved centuries ago. 'See how intricate they are?'

We made our way to the countess's bedchamber, and Zara let out an awed gasp. The grand four-poster bed dominated the room. As she wandered around the chamber, examining various artefacts and furniture, a shimmery figure appeared in the tall mirror. She jumped back, startled by its sudden appearance.

Charlotte stepped through into the room, her bustling dress flowing around her. 'Who is it goes thither?'

'This is Zara,' I told the countess. 'She might work here. At the moment, I'm giving her a quick private tour.'

Charlotte smiled. 'Ah, a pleasure 'tis to greet thee, Zara. I am Charlotte of Chirtle, formerly its countess in times past.'

'It's nice to meet you, too,' Zara said, recovering from the surprise.

'Welcome to this estate, young one. Peradventure thee shalt spy me hither and yon—ofttimes startling the onlookers.' She smirked.

Zara thanked her before we left the bedchamber and continued our tour.

When Lydia and Penny's cars spit gravel in the car park, we headed downstairs to welcome them inside.

I could tell Zara was already smitten with Chirtlewood, the ghosts she'd met and the stories I'd told her of its past inhabitants. I smiled; she would be a quick learner and a useful addition to the staff.

If she stayed. If she could be trusted working here.

We met Lydia and Penny in the small office we shared.

'Ladies,' I said, ushering Zara forward. 'This is Zara. She expressed an interest in working here. I showed her around. I hope that was all right.'

'Of course.' Lydia studied Zara for a few moments. Lines of concern creased her forehead. Maybe she was uneasy about how young Zara was compared to the rest of us.

'Nice to meet you,' Penny said, but I could tell by the lack of emotion in her voice she wasn't entirely genuine.

'Well, then... shall we sit and eat?' I suggested.

We all took a seat at the table. I ripped open the paper bags of pastries. Croissants and blueberry tarts appeared, their freshly baked aroma making my mouth water.

But instead of picking up a treat, I spoke to Lydia. I needed a way and a time to bring up this conversation, and this was it.

'Lydia, have you heard anything new from Inspector Pentecost about... you know?'

She shook her head while stuffing her mouth with a flaky croissant.

'The detective?' Penny said. 'Are you still investigating mysteries?'

'Yes,' Lydia said with her mouth full. 'The woman who drowned in the river in Richmond.'

'This might surprise you.' I glanced over at Zara before continuing. 'I found out last night that Zara is Jane Middlemore's daughter.'

Lydia sprayed a few pastry flakes across the table, while Penny's tart-filled hand stopped halfway to her mouth. 'What?' they exclaimed in unison.

Zara shot me a sharp look. 'How did you find that out?'

'Your father told me last night.' I shrugged nonchalantly and grabbed a croissant.

She squirmed back into her seat awkwardly, letting her pastry fall to the table. 'He shouldn't have.'

'Her funeral is this morning,' Penny blurted out. 'Didn't you know?'

Lydia and I both glared at Penny. Clearly, Lydia had the same thought as me. Zara might not even know of her mother's untimely death.

'I'm not going,' Zara said. She exhaled. 'My mother and I didn't get on.'

Well, *that* mystery was solved. She *did* know of Jane's death.

Lydia turned back to Zara. 'We met your mother once. She was a... unique person.'

A dry laugh escaped Zara's lips. 'That's a fucking understatement.'

'Do you have a photo of you and your mum?' I asked. 'I'd love to see it.'

Lydia caught my eye. 'Me too,' she said.

'Why do you want to see that?' Zara asked.

So, she did have a photo. But would she show it to us?

Lydia shrugged. 'We're midlife romantics. We'd like to see how close a resemblance you are to her, see if you looked happy... that's all.'

Zara sighed. 'Fine. I've got one here.' She pulled a purse from a deep pocket of her coat, opened it and withdrew a photo, which she placed on the table between Lydia and me.

The bottom quarter of the photo had been torn away.

Lydia lifted her head. Our eyes met. I'm sure we had the same question. Did the partial photograph the inspector had found match the missing part of this one?

'Not much of a likeness,' Penny said, leaning over to peer at the photograph. 'Not from what I can tell, anyway. Were you adopted?'

'No.' Zara snatched the photo away and stuffed it into her purse.

'We ought to get started,' Penny said. 'Look at the time.'

'Yes,' I said. 'Zara, why don't you come with me? We'll start preparing the house for visitors, and then station ourselves at the front desk to sell tickets.'

'Sounds good,' Zara replied.

We stood. I caught Lydia's gaze again with a meaningful look. For dramatic effect, I even raised an eyebrow.

'I need to make a quick call first,' Lydia said. 'Then I'll join you all.'

And with that, we scattered in different directions to complete our tasks before the tourists descended on the manor.

Zara and I roamed the house, checking each room to make sure everything was tidy and nothing was amiss. I didn't make conversation. One thought pounded in my head: Zara has a photo of her and Abaddon and Jane *with one corner torn off*. Was the partial photo I found on the riverbank the missing piece to Zara's family snapshot? If it was, that would place her at the scene of the crime.

I hadn't seen the torn-off corner closely enough to be sure it was a perfect match. But what would be the chance that it wasn't? Slim, right?

Maybe Zara was the person seen walking with Jane along the riverbank. But then what happened?

'Heather, you're awfully quiet,' Zara commented as we came back downstairs.

'Just enjoying the peace before the tourists arrive in droves,' I lied.

Chapter 34

AT THE FRONT DESK, we had barely finished exchanging pleasantries with our first visitors of the day when Inspector Pentecost strode in the entrance.

'Good morning, Heather.'

'Morning, Inspector.' I gestured to Zara, who was standing with me behind the ticketing desk. 'This is Zara, Jane Middlemore's daughter.'

Zara shot me a confused glance, then faced the inspector. 'What's going on?' she asked hesitantly.

The inspector paused before answering her. 'I must ask you to come with me to the police station for questioning. It's in connection with your mother's death.'

Zara's eyes widened. 'What? No!' she shouted and took a step back from the desk, her eyes wide.

'I understand; however, it is necessary you come with me so we can investigate the matter further with your help.'

'But why?' Zara protested. 'What do you need me for? I haven't done anything!'

'We can discuss that at the station,' Inspector Pentecost said calmly.

I put a hand on Zara's shoulder in an attempt to calm her. She seemed frozen in place. 'It's all right, Zara,' I said as I gently turned her towards the door. 'It's probably routine. Go with the inspector.'

Zara's eyes flicked between us before she walked out the door. The inspector and I followed close behind. As we left the house, Zara yelled out a final protest:

'This is crazy! You have no proof that I had anything to do with my mother's death!'

She bolted towards the river.

For what? To find a getaway boat, somewhere to hide, a spot to throw herself in? It was impossible to guess.

Inspector Pentecost didn't hesitate. She tore off in pursuit, arms pumping like an athlete in a sprint race.

I briefly considered joining the chase. I'd recovered well from my hysterectomy, and I'd regained a lot of my fitness. But Zara was nearly thirty years younger and had a good head start. I'd never catch her.

Instead, I made the witchy sign on my hand and reached out one arm. I concentrated fiercely, remembering what had happened with the mirror at the train station and in my demonstration to Rachel. Magic at my command, when I wanted it.

Wind. Give me wind.

As Zara ran, the leaves and dirt around her feet flew up and swirled around her legs. It was as if she were running in a mini tornado. A few moments later, she stumbled to the ground and rolled.

I ran down the steps of Chirtlewood's entrance and onto the manicured lawn, my heart pounding.

Zara sat up. She glared and thrust out her hands. An invisible force barged me on the shoulder, and I tumbled to the ground.

So, she could respond in kind.

Zara scrambled to her feet, but the inspector was closing in on her. As she turned to run, the inspector reached out a hand and grabbed her by the arm.

Oh no. Now the inspector will get a taste of Zara's magic.

I was wrong. Inspector Pentecost, with the expert dexterity of someone who had done this many times, twisted Zara's arm behind her back. Within seconds, she had handcuffed the young girl.

I got to my feet, breathing heavily, brushing off dirt and leaves. The fall had winded me.

The inspector's voice carried on the breeze as she arrested Zara, reading her the Miranda rights and admonishing her for bolting.

Lydia ran over and joined me with a concerned expression. 'Are you okay? I saw you fall.'

'I didn't fall,' I said, rubbing my sore arm. 'Zara's magic shoved me over.'

'Really? I hope you got her back.'

'No, I got her first.' I grinned.

We fell silent as the inspector approached, holding Zara firmly by the arm. The girl had stopped struggling. Her head hung low, and her mouth was turned down, resigned to her fate.

With her other hand, Inspector Pentecost pulled a small plastic bag from a pocket of her jacket. It contained the torn corner of the photo she'd retrieved from the riverbank.

'Does this look like the missing piece for the photo you saw?' she asked.

Lydia leaned closer to check it out. 'That's the torn-off part. I'm sure of it.'

I agreed.

'Thank you. I'll get statements from you two ladies later. Right now, I'll take this one to the station for processing.'

'Inspector, there's something else you should know,' I said. 'Remember the footprint near the river? Zara was wearing muddy boots when she arrived at my aunt's house on the evening of the murder. Once we learned who she truly was and identified her motive—that she hated and blamed her mother for failing her—everything clicked into place.'

'Fuck you all,' Zara said. 'You couldn't know what it was like to grow up living with that woman. She made my life hell every day.'

'Tell us at the station,' the inspector said. She marched Zara towards her car, but turned back as if a new thought had struck her.

'There's something strange about you two,' she said. 'I don't know what it is, but I want to talk to you about it sometime. Soon. And if you don't spill the beans, I'll figure it out. I promise you that.'

I frowned. The inspector wouldn't forget about this. How long could I pretend there wasn't anything supernatural going on? Maybe not long. And if I did put her off track, she would press Lydia for information. Sooner or later, we might have to let the inspector in on the secret of our witchy powers. Otherwise, she would mistrust us.

'Goodbye, Inspector,' Lydia called.

'Thanks for your help.' She turned and escorted Zara to her car.

We watched her drive off before we turned to go back inside.

Penny was standing at the front entrance, her mouth agape. 'That young girl killed her own mother? How could anyone do such a thing?'

'Awful, isn't it?' The idea of such an unspeakable act made me ill.

'It's unbelievable,' Lydia said.

We fell silent, sharing a minute or two of contemplation.

Finally, Lydia spoke up. 'We've got tourists here. We need to look after them, so we'd better get back to work.'

'What about Jane's funeral?' I asked. 'Shouldn't one of us go?'

Lydia frowned. 'We didn't know her.'

'I expect there will be very few people there.' Abaddon. Maybe her neighbour. 'It seems like the right thing to do.'

'You're right. Go on, then. Penny and I will manage until you get back.'

'Thanks. I appreciate it.'

THE FUNERAL WAS IN half an hour, in Richmond. I'd best leave Chirtlewood straight away, so I didn't get caught up with talking to a group of tourists whom I couldn't get away from. I grabbed my bag from the office and headed out to the car.

I hesitated before turning the ignition key, apprehensive thoughts running through my mind. What would Abaddon think of me being there? Might he consider it an intrusion? Soon, the police will notify him that his daughter killed his ex-wife. How furious will he be when he finds out I helped bring her to justice?

After a few minutes of prevaricating, I stopped worrying about how Abaddon might react to my presence at the funeral. I should do what I needed to do. And that was to show my respects to a woman who'd been in my thoughts recently, who needed help but never received it, tragically meeting a cruel end at the hands of a guest staying with my aunt and me.

With newfound determination, I started the car and drove off.

'About time. I wast beginning to bethink thee hadst succumbed to sleep!' Charlotte said from behind me.

I jumped in my seat and spun around.

The countess and the earl had squeezed into the back seat.

'If thou art not travelling too far, we wouldst like to accompany thee,' Charlotte said with an air of entitlement.

'Um... Only to Richmond. To a funeral.'

'Aye, that is wherefore we wanted to wend. 'Twill be a pleasant outing for us. We can socialise and catch up on recent news.'

'Socialise with who? Other ghosts?'

'Aye,' the earl said. ''Tis a special occasion. Wouldn't miss it. Thee can't beat a good funeral. Though 'twast hard to keep up with them all during the bubonic plague.'

I could imagine. There might even be more ghosts than people there.

'Whose funeral is it? Anyone we might know?' Charlotte asked.

'A local woman, Jane Middlemore. A witch. She visited the house recently.' I left out the part about her stealing things from our kitchen.

'Hast nay clue who is this chit,' the earl mused. 'I suppose thither shall be enow people to make it bearable. And at least the weather is clement. Nay need for me to suffer through a rainstorm.'

'She drowned,' I said. 'We believe her daughter deliberately pushed her into the river.'

Charlotte gasped. 'How awful! Pray tell, hath the naughty daughter been sent to the Tower for her treacherous deed?'

'No.' I sighed. 'Nowadays, we have a modern judicial system that doesn't involve locking people in the Tower of London until their punishment is meted out in a deadly manner.'

'Thither's nothing wrong with the occasional public execution,' the earl said. 'It provides a spectacle for onlookers and does tend to deter other miscreants.'

'I don't want to debate it,' I exclaimed, taking a corner a little too fast. Could I get to Richmond any sooner? This conversation was far too macabre for me.

I pulled up outside the small church where Jane Middlemore's funeral service would be held. 'Look, we're here.'

We exited the car and entered the church. The interior was dimly lit, and it smelled musty.

Abaddon sat in the front row of pews, alone. I considered joining him, but I doubted he'd welcome my presence, so I sat at the back. No one else was present except for the priest. A pang of sadness hit me, like when I noticed there was nothing to commemorate Jane's passing at the riverbank. Few, if any, people cared about her.

No one else living was present, that is. Many ghosts stood gathered in clusters in the shadows deep along the walls, chatting amongst themselves like old friends reuniting after years apart.

I'd always wondered why it seemed cold at funerals. Now I knew. It was the chill of death seeping forth from a multitude of ghosts hanging out together.

The service was brief. The priest spoke kindly of Jane, then contemplated Abaddon expectantly, as if to invite him to say a few words himself. The warlock remained where he was, his head down.

When the service was over, I quickly slipped out before he saw me.

Unfortunately, Charlotte and the earl didn't follow me. They must have been having too much fun socialising.

I waited in the car as it heated up in the sun. Abaddon left the church and plodded away without noticing me.

After a while, the Chirtlewood ghosts emerged and piled into the back seat.

They continued to chatter, but I remained silent, my head swimming with upsetting thoughts. I drove us back to Chirtlewood.

Chapter 35

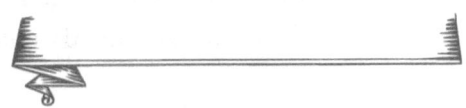

INSPECTOR PENTECOST phoned later in the day to tell us that, once Zara had been presented with the incontrovertible evidence against her, she'd confessed to pushing her mother into the river and leaving her there. She hadn't intended for her mother to drown.

In turn, I told her that Zara's father, Abaddon Masana, was staying at my aunt's house. The inspector said she would go to speak with him personally.

So, after Chirtlewood closed for the day, I drove home in a daze. I'd called Abaddon for help with Aunt Ruth's mirror, and he'd sent Zara in his place. Zara killed her mother. I'd put the entire sequence into motion. Would Jane Middlemore still be alive if I hadn't made that call?

A chill reverberated in my bones, even though it was warm in the car. Did I bear any responsibility for this tragic turn of events?

No, it wasn't my fault. I couldn't have known what was going to happen. I'd done nothing wrong.

When I arrived home, I greeted Aunt Ruth and Raven. They were poring over an enormous book at the kitchen table. Ghastly green steam rose from a pot on the hob. I hoped it wasn't dinner.

'We're making up the healing potion,' Aunt Ruth explained.

'Okay. Great.' They were using the spell book we'd copied. 'Let's get a takeaway tonight, then.' I held my breath and went out to the back garden, where I could see Abaddon sitting alone, staring into nothingness.

I went up to him, making sure my footsteps were not so quiet that I'd catch him by surprise. He'd had enough shocks for one day.

'Abaddon?' I whispered.

He didn't move. 'Good evening, Heather.' His voice was low and quiet.

'Zara used to sit here, at this exact spot,' I said, sitting on the lawn beside him.

'I sensed that,' he said, finally meeting my gaze.

'I'm so sorry about what happened,' I said.

'It was a tragic accident. Zara was angry. She lashed out at her mother in frustration.'

I said nothing. No one but Zara would ever know for certain what her intentions had been that evening.

'She regretted it,' Abaddon continued. 'That's why she punished herself. At the time, I thought she was doing it because she'd failed to help you with the spell book and the mirror.'

Wait, what? 'She punished herself? How?'

'She cast a simple spell on my walking cane so it would hit her. I should have stopped it, but I was too confused by what she was doing. And then your aunt and your friend threw me out of the house before I could explain.'

Oh no. All this time, Raven and I had mistakenly believed it was the warlock who had cast the spell to punish Zara with his cane. We thought he wanted a potion of forgiveness to absolve himself of the guilt for that act. Instead, Zara had cast the spell to animate the cane to hit herself.

My mind raced as I processed everything. Abaddon must have found out that Zara was the cause of Jane's death. She must have told Abaddon about it, leading to the huge argument we heard. Then they both kept this awful secret to themselves. That's why he hadn't denied using magic on his cane to hit Zara. If he'd said Zara had done it herself, we would have asked questions, and he didn't want us to pry into it.

Abaddon hadn't been seeking forgiveness for himself after all. He'd wanted a potion to help himself forgive Zara for what she had done. And then he'd generously given it to her in the hope that it would free her from the torment of her guilt.

My heart sank with shame. I should not have been so quick to judge him or his intentions. 'I'm so sorry, Abaddon,' I whispered. 'I badly misjudged you. Can you forgive me?' Ouch. That question was a faux pas.

He nodded sadly, yet still managed a small smile of appreciation for my apology. 'Thank you. There's no need to apologise. I understand completely. Don't worry about Zara. I'll make sure she gets all the best legal and psychological help there is.'

'I'm here for you if you ever need anything.'

We stayed there in silence for a while, watching the stars appear one by one and twinkle softly in the twilight sky. Eventually, Abaddon got up without a word and went inside, and I followed him.

A FEW MINUTES LATER, Aunt Ruth wheeled herself into the living room with a sparkle in her eyes. 'Heather, I did it! I've created the healing potion. My magic mirror is fully recharged. Everything's ready for me to take it.'

'Wait a minute. Are there any risks involved in taking this potion?'

She waved her hand dismissively. 'It's perfectly safe. The orchids used in the recipe are harmless to humans.'

'Good. But, Aunt Ruth, I don't understand why you needed your mirror fixed before you could try healing yourself? Isn't the potion enough?'

She chuckled, almost as if she expected that question. 'The powdered orchids have healing properties, but I need the mirror to boost their magical energy for the potion. Without it, the potion would be little more than a small, green smoothie with a foul taste. It wouldn't have the power to heal me.'

'Ah, right. Got it. So, are you going to drink the potion now? I must see this.'

'Not yet. Abaddon suggested I wait until midnight. It will be more potent then.'

Midnight. The witching hour. That made sense.

'Sounds great.' Excitement grew within me. I could walk on clouds.

Aunt Ruth looked around. 'Where is Abaddon, anyway?'

'I think he went to bed. It's been a bloody horrendous day for him.'

'A festering bedevilment of a day, for sure.'

Raven came into the room. 'I've tidied up. Now, I guess we have nothing to do but wait until midnight.' He spoke slowly, in a monotone.

I smiled at Raven. His struggle to keep his enthusiasm under control was palpable. The moment he let it flow free, his curse would trigger, and he'd fly off into the night in raven form... yet again.

We all wanted Aunt Ruth to fully recover from her fall, regain movement in her legs, and return to her old self. The doctors had warned her it was unlikely, but not impossible.

No matter how much we wished for it, no improvement had come naturally. We all believed that only magic would help her now.

So, we waited, perched in our seats like storks in their telephone pole nests. Time dragged on agonisingly. My heart beat to the rhythm of the seconds and minutes ticking away on the clock. Tension in the air grew like electrical energy in a thundercloud.

At last, midnight struck and we all rushed into the kitchen.

Earlier, Raven had propped the ancient, ornate mirror against the wall. On the kitchen table sat a glass filled with a shimmering green potion. I shuddered at the unbidden thought of a random insect having flown into the concoction while it sat there for hours, but the liquid was untainted.

Aunt Ruth placed her palms on both the mirror and the glass containing the potion. A dazzling light reflected and refracted off them both like a million tiny green gems.

'The potion is magically charged now,' she said with a subtle calm.

'Drink it,' Raven said, his eyes wide and hopeful.

Aunt Ruth downed the potion in a single gulp, her face contorting in disgust at its taste.

Nothing happened. My heart sank with dread. I searched her face for signs of change in case I was wrong. 'How do you feel?' I demanded, a tremor in my voice. 'Did it work?'

She turned towards me and smiled. Her teeth were emerald green, as if she'd been eating spinach soup. 'Not any different yet. It might take a while. Abaddon said as much.'

'How long?' Raven asked, his forehead furrowed in concern.

'Perhaps a week, maybe less.'

My head throbbed. The pressure of the past few days was taking a toll. And now we wouldn't know for days if the potion would be successful.

Chapter 36

THREE DAYS LATER, I went to Richmond Park for a walk after work.

It was an immense area. I parked in one of the car parks and set off for Isabella Plantation, a beautiful, enclosed, botanical garden in the centre of the park. I'd discovered this stunning oasis of flowers and trees only recently, and I loved exploring it whenever I could. It was like an enchanted garden from a fairy tale, minus the fairies.

I skirted around a small wood, where the shrieks of ring-necked parakeets overpowered every other sound, including the traffic on the A3 and the planes descending to Heathrow Airport every ninety seconds. The green birds had taken over most of Richmond Park.

I emerged into a rolling grassland area. In the distance, a herd of deer grazed contentedly. They were the reason the plantation was so well fenced.

My fitness level had increased immeasurably since I'd started walking. The evenings were light until 9 pm at this time of year, and there were plenty of people about with the same idea as me. Some of them were running, though. I'd stick with walking.

My thoughts swirled with the chaos of the past few days. Abaddon had gone home the day after Jane's funeral. Aunt Ruth, Raven and I were still desperately waiting to see if the healing potion would work. The inspector had phoned to tell me that Zara had been charged with manslaughter. Lydia, and now Penny, as well as the Chirtlewood ghosts, wanted to know when we could investigate another mystery, as if they thought I could fabricate them at will.

Zara. I thought I'd connected with her. I thought I was helping her get away from a tyrant. But she'd lied about her past—perhaps about much more than that. She'd killed her mother and then turned up at Aunt Ruth's house a short time later as if nothing had happened. She'd told the inspector that she didn't know her mother couldn't swim, but did I believe her? I wasn't sure.

Abaddon. Aunt Ruth had warned me not to trust the powerful warlock. Of course, I did trust him at first. Later, I believed he was tricking us. All that sneaking around at midnight to pick orchids for him, but he'd planned ahead so he could prepare the petals for the healing potion for Aunt Ruth. The times he was irritable or grumpy, and he was hiding the fact that his only daughter had killed his ex-wife. I'd thought he was mean and untrustworthy, but instead he was hurting and doing his best to help us in difficult circumstances.

For several days, I'd supposed Zara was someone I could trust, someone I could form a bond with. Abaddon was someone I didn't like and didn't trust. But it turned out to be the opposite.

I needed to work on my perception of people. Or maybe be a little less judgemental and trusting of others until I truly got to know them.

My phone pinged with a text message when I was almost at the gate for Isabella Plantation.

Raven: *Come home quickly!*

What's wrong? I phoned him back immediately, but it went directly to voicemail.

Shit. What's happened? Why wouldn't he answer?

I called Ruth. She didn't answer either. This wasn't good.

By this time, I'd turned and was marching back to my car. No, that would take too long. I picked up the pace and started a slow jog through the park. Several deer turned to gaze at me curiously before they returned to their grazing.

My knee would kill me tomorrow for this physical exertion, but I had to get home as fast as I could. My throat tightened. What if Aunt Ruth had suffered another accident?

The shrieking parakeets seemed to be either berating me or urging me on, as if I was in the last mile of a marathon.

I reached the car park with sweat pouring off my face. My damp top clung uncomfortably to my skin.

I drove through the park and out Kingston Gate and towards home. What had happened? No one had called me back. I'd left messages for them both.

I skidded into the driveway, the tyres kicking gravel every which way. Abandoning the car with the door open, I sprinted into the house.

'Raven! Aunt Ruth!' I shouted from the entrance hall, my voice echoing through the house.

'In here, Heather,' Aunt Ruth called from the kitchen.

I dashed in. Aunt Ruth sat calmly at the kitchen table, sipping a cup of tea. She smiled.

She appeared to be all right. I sighed, partly with relief, partly with exhaustion.

'Raven messaged me and told me to come home. I thought something was wrong, that maybe you were hurt.'

'No, I'm fine. Nothing wrong with me.'

'Where's Raven?'

'Flying over Kingston somewhere, I expect.'

Oh no. His curse had kicked in again. Maybe right after he'd messaged me. That would explain why he hadn't answered when I called him back.

'What happened?' Something must have happened. Something bad. I glanced around the kitchen. Everything seemed to be in place. And the living room had appeared normal too. The entrance hall—

Now I remembered. I'd rushed past Aunt Ruth's wheelchair beside the front door. Then how did she—

Aunt Ruth grinned and stood. She took a step. Then another. She strode forward and embraced me.

'I can walk again!' she said. 'The potion worked. And I couldn't have done it without everything you did for me, Heather. You're the most wonderful niece in the world.'

I couldn't reply. I was so lost for words. Tears of happiness streamed down my face, mixing with the sweat.

'It's been a tough week,' Aunt Ruth said, 'but it was worth it. Sadly, Raven got so excited at the sight of me walking that it triggered his curse.'

'We'll have to find a way to lift that burden from him, Aunt Ruth.'

'Oh, we will, somehow. Not that we haven't been trying.'

We disengaged from our hug and I wiped my face.

'And look,' Aunt Ruth added, pointing at a letter on the table. 'If I'm not mistaken, that's the letter from the witchy correspondence course you've been waiting for. If you've passed—and I'm sure you would have—you can move on to the practical assignments next.' Although, thanks to my aunt, I was already starting to understand my magic.

'I'll read it later. Right now, I'm so excited that you can walk again I can't focus on anything else!'

'Yeah, me too.' She beamed with joy.

'Now you're recovered, there's another important matter,' I said. 'September the third.'

'I told you not to concern yourself with that,' she replied, an edge to her voice.

'You told me it will be the date you die! How can I not worry about it?' Anxiety rose in my throat.

Aunt Ruth walked to the window and stared out at the garden, keeping her face averted. 'I'm sorry. I shouldn't have said anything. I had a weak moment. It's something I must deal with myself.'

'It doesn't work that way. We're family. I'll help you with whatever it is. But you need to talk to me. Tell me what's important about September the third. Tell me why you believe you'll die that day.'

For a long moment, Aunt Ruth was silent. Then she swivelled to face me. 'All right. I will tell you. In the coming days.'

'You promise?'

She nodded, but her eyes held an expression of sadness. 'Go on, open your letter, Heather. Let's see what it says.'

I stepped over to the table and picked up the letter. A letter opener was around somewhere, but I wasn't going to waste time looking for that. I tore the envelope open with my fingers, revealing a thick, cream-coloured letter.

I pulled it out, dropping the envelope onto the table. Holding my breath, I unfolded the letter with my eyes closed.

'What does it say?' Curiosity spiked Aunt Ruth's voice.

I opened my eyes. My gaze was drawn to the words centred at the top of the letter: *Congratulations! You have passed with distinction.*

'Yes!' I fist-pumped. 'I'm a fully-fledged apprentice witch now!'

'Well done,' Aunt Ruth chuckled. 'I told you there wasn't anything to worry about.'

About the Author

Raven Raine is the pen name of a reclusive author in New Zealand who writes **Paranormal Women's Fiction**.

I live with my partner, two children and two cats. I write by a window with a beautiful cherry blossom tree spread out before me, a steaming cup of coffee on the desk within easy reach, and the grating sound of cat claws on the furniture in the room behind. Frequently, one of the cats will sit on the desk or keyboard while I try to write.

Read more at https://ravenraine.com.

www.ingramcontent.com/pod-product-compliance
Lightning Source LLC
Chambersburg PA
CBHW020052180626
46812CB00006B/2297